Someone had tricked her into coming to the reunion, Amber realized.

Someone who wanted to make sure I'd be here.

"Amber? Are you okay?" Caleb asked.

He was staring at her, an eyebrow lifted in concern. Before she could formulate a response, a scream pierced the silence.

She shot to her feet. The scream had come from outside.

Caleb brushed past Amber at a full run before dropping to the stone walkway beside the body on the ground.

When Amber reached them, she stifled a gasp. The victim was Alex. From their old group of friends.

Caleb held up a hand. "Everyone stay back."

She stepped forward and knelt beside him. *Everyone* didn't include her. "I'm a cop."

Amber drew in a shaky breath. First Mona, now Alex. One-third of them gone before age thirty.

"This is Detective Caleb Sutherland with the Levy County Sheriff's Office." Caleb spoke into the phone, his voice all cool professionalism. *Detective? Caleb?*

She figured he'd be a preacher or something equally righteous. Now they'd work together to solve this murder.

Murders.

Carol J. Post writes fun and fast-paced inspirational romantic suspense stories and lives in sunshiny central Florida. She sings and plays the piano for her church and also enjoys sailing, hiking, camping—almost anything outdoors. Her daughters and grandkids live too far away for her liking, so she now pours all that nurturing into taking care of two fat and sassy cats and one highly spoiled dachshund.

Books by Carol J. Post

Love Inspired Suspense

REUNITED BY DANGER

CAROL J. POST

HARLEQUIN® LOVE INSPIRED® SUSPENSE

Recycling programs
for this product may
not exist in your area.

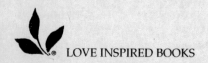

LOVE INSPIRED BOOKS

ISBN-13: 978-0-373-67848-8

Reunited by Danger

www.Harlequin.com

Printed in U.S.A.

As far as the east is from the west,
so far has He removed our transgressions from us.
–Psalms 103:12

Acknowledgments

Thank you to all the people who supported me in writing this series:

All the helpful people on Cedar Key.

My wonderful critique partners,
Karen Fleming and Sabrina Jarema.

My awesome editor, Giselle Regus.

My lovely agent, Nalini Akolekar.

My sweet, supportive family.

And my loving husband.

You are the best!

ONE

Just three hours and it would be over.

Amber Kingston slid into a chair at an empty table and watched the colorful crush of bodies gyrating on the dance floor. A banner hung over the stage: *10-Year Reunion* in gold and blue letters. The music of Linkin Park blasted through the speakers at a volume capable of shattering glass.

Amber observed the activity from her solitary perch in the back, thankful for a few moments alone. This wasn't how she'd wanted to spend her Saturday night. She'd come because of Ramona, who she hadn't talked to in almost ten years. Who, a month ago, sent her a Facebook message out of the blue, begging her to come to this stupid high school reunion. Mona had said she was dying of cancer and had six months to live. She didn't want to be remembered as the girl she'd been in high school.

Actually, Amber didn't, either.

The music faded and another song grew to full volume within seconds. Ramona had twisted her arm to get her there and hadn't even shown up.

"Fancy seeing you here."

The male voice close to her ear drew her gaze to the smiling face behind it. He'd slipped into the event space from a side door.

She returned the smile. "Caleb."

He eased into the chair next to her. Though the planes of his face had matured, his eyes were still the same Caribbean Sea blue. Sandy-blond hair fell in soft layers. Little had changed since high school, but he'd acquired some mass over the past ten years, the kind that came from hard work rather than too much Southern cooking.

He leaned toward her, the closeness necessary for conversation. He even smelled nice, a light citrusy scent with hints of spice. "I hope it's all right if I join you."

"Totally."

Caleb Lyons had always been nice to her. Of course, he'd been nice to everybody. Defender of the underdog. He'd lived four doors down. They'd even gone to the same church for a while. Other than that, their circles had rarely intersected, although they were in the same grade. His gang was filled with the good kids——band members, chess club participants, straight-A students, kids who never missed Sunday school or youth group because they *wanted* to be there. Back then she'd been sure their sole purpose in life was to make her and her friends look bad.

He propped an elbow on the table and rested his chin in his hand. "What are you up to these days? Still living in Florida?"

"I'm a cop for Cedar Key."

He threw back his head and laughed, the sound carrying over the decibels pounding from the speakers. After slapping his hand on the table a couple of times, he shook his head, still chuckling. "I'm sorry. I knew you'd have dealings with the police, but that wasn't the kind I expected."

The grin he flashed her tugged one out of her. "What can I say? I finally got some sense." Fortunately she'd acquired it before any of her stupid shenanigans made it onto her adult record.

Growing up with two older brothers who were polar opposites, she'd always thought Harold's daredevil lifestyle looked more exciting than Hunter's straitlaced ways. Good thing she'd wised up when she had. Now Hunter was serving the people of Cedar Key alongside her, and Harold was a long-time resident of Florida State. The prison, not the school.

The music faded and the DJ took the microphone.

"Y'all having a great time?"

Shouts echoed throughout the room. After welcoming everyone, his tone turned somber.

"There are four classmates who are no longer with us. Let's remember each with a moment of silence."

Amber knew about the first death. It had happened two days after graduation, a murder that had rocked the small town of Chiefland. The next two names were familiar. Both had died in their early twenties. Amber didn't know them well, but sadness wove through her anyway. The other guests apparently felt it, too. Silence hung over the room, a stark contrast to the noise that had shaken the walls less than five minutes earlier.

The DJ continued. "Lastly, in April of this year, we lost Ramona Freeborn."

Amber's jaw dropped as the words slammed into her. *Ramona died two months ago.*

So who'd sent the Facebook message in May, pretending to be Mona? And the follow-up ones, as recently as last weekend, confirming she hadn't changed her mind about coming to the reunion?

Someone who wanted to make sure I'd be here.

The temperature in the room dropped. Or maybe the chill was internal.

"Amber? Are you okay?" Caleb sat staring at her, an eyebrow lifted in concern. Before she could formulate a response, a scream pierced the silence.

She shot to her feet, snatching her purse from the table. The scream had come from outside. Another followed it. She dashed to the nearest exit with a handful of other people. The others remained glued to their seats, their eyes wide and jaws lax.

She soon located the source of the commotion. A woman stood in the glow of the garden lights, hands pressed to her mouth. Shivers racked her body and wails escaped between her fingers.

Olivia Chamberlain. Liv. They'd been the best of friends—Amber, Liv and Mona, along with Alex, Vince and Ray—until they'd all racked up growing lists of misdemeanors and increasingly serious alcohol addictions. And a dead body.

Caleb brushed past her at a full run before dropping to the stone walkway in front of Liv. Someone was on the ground.

When Amber reached them, Caleb had his

cell phone pressed to his ear. She stifled a gasp. Alex O'Dell.

Caleb held up a hand. "Everyone stay back."

She knelt beside him. *Everyone* didn't include her. "I'm a cop." She cast the words over her shoulder and then grasped her former friend's wrist to check for a pulse. Nothing. Judging from the awkward angle of Alex's head, his neck was broken. Blood trickled from the corner of his mouth. Another small trail came from his nose, both combining to form a darkening oval on the garden pavers.

Amber drew in a shaky breath. Mona, now Alex. One-third of them gone before age thirty.

"This is Detective Caleb Lyons with the Levy County Sheriff's Office," Caleb spoke into the phone, his voice all cool professionalism.

Detective? Caleb? She figured he'd be a preacher or something equally righteous.

He continued with the same somber tone. "We have a homicide."

Several gasps sounded around them. "He was murdered?"

Amber looked up at the former cheerleader who'd spoken. "Any suspicious death is investigated as a homicide until foul play is ruled out."

Alex had apparently fallen. Or been pushed. Her gaze followed the side of the stucco building to a curved balcony, its wrought-iron railing thirteen or fourteen feet up. Situated halfway between Chiefland and Bronson, the Mediterranean Revival-style structure had likely been someone's home. But during her lifetime, it had been a venue for weddings and other events. Tonight, Amber hadn't gone upstairs. Their group had booked only the bottom floor.

So what had Alex been doing up there?

She straightened and draped her arm across Liv's shoulders. The wails had quieted to sniffles, but shivers still shook her body.

"Did you see what happened?"

Liv shook her head. "I hadn't been here long."

Amber nodded. That would explain why they hadn't seen each other.

Liv continued. "It was so crowded inside, I came out here to be alone. That's when I found him."

Amber scanned those gathered. Other classmates were now filing out of the building. The police would need to talk to all of them. Of course, almost everyone had been inside, like her, and probably hadn't seen anything.

As she studied the faces around her, one man snagged her gaze. He was standing to the side. The glow of the garden lights didn't reach his face, but she didn't need to see him to know he was watching her. She could feel it. The hostility rolling toward her was almost palpable.

Logan Cleary. Anytime she came back to Chiefland, she tried to avoid him. Although she hadn't been ready to leave her friends, moving to Ocala right after graduation had been a relief.

"He blames us, you know."

Amber started at hearing a new voice close to her ear and frowned at Vince Mahoney. "He blames *me*."

"He blames all of us."

She crossed her arms, warding off a sudden chill in spite of the balmy June night. Vince and the others were part of the gang, but she was the one who'd sent the texts, inviting Logan's brother to join them at their hangout in the woods. Landon Cleary had been a class-A jerk. But even after she'd learned the truth, she hadn't wanted him dead.

She dropped her arm from Liv's shoulders and cast a glance at Alex. Caleb was doing a good job of preserving the scene. No one had ventured near the body. She started to turn away then hesitated. Something white was caught in the branches of a shrub a few feet from where Alex lay. Paper? She pressed her purse against her side, unease chewing at the edges of her mind.

When she'd been in the bathroom earlier,

someone had slid a sheet of paper, folded in quarters, under the stall door. Black sequined ballet slippers and a hand covered by a black silk glove were all she'd seen. No one at the reunion was wearing either.

She put a hand on Vince's arm. "Did someone give you a sheet of paper tonight?"

His eyes widened, providing the answer before he opened his mouth. "I was standing at the bar talking to someone. When I went to pick up my drink, a sheet of paper was sitting next to it."

Raymond Ellis staggered up to join them. Not much had changed. He was as wasted as he'd been when they'd hung out in high school.

She turned her attention to Vince. "What did the paper say?"

"'All of life's pleasures surround you.'" He studied her. "You got one, too."

She nodded. "'A sworn public servant, you've answered the call.'"

"You're a cop."

It wasn't a secret. When she'd first arrived, she'd caught up with everyone except Liv, and they'd filled each other in on their lives. Raymond worked as a mechanic in a tire-and-lube place, and Alex was a trim carpenter. Vince had scored big. He'd married into money and had a cushy management job in his father-in-law's manufacturing business. He was probably enjoying some of those pleasures mentioned in his note.

Ray squinted at them. "What are you talking about?"

"Someone slipped us notes," Amber said. "One line about each of our lives."

"I didn't get anything." After patting his back pockets, Ray produced a piece of paper. His brows drew together. "I didn't know I had this." After unfolding the single page, he read it aloud. "'Once you were bound, but now you're free.'"

Vince wrinkled his nose. "What's that supposed to mean?"

Ray had suddenly sobered up. "I did a couple years for drug charges. Not many people know about it. I was living in Georgia."

Amber turned. "Liv?"

Liv spun around, eyes filled with panic. "My purse. I had it when I came into the garden."

Amber put a hand on her shoulder. "You probably dropped it when you found Alex. I'm sure it's here somewhere."

Sirens sounded in the distance, gradually increasing in volume. When the police arrived, the contents of those notes were going into the report, regardless of what her friends wanted.

Caleb approached and handed Liv a black clutch. "It was under a bush."

She snapped open the small bag and looked inside. "I have no idea who put this in here."

"Wait." Amber held up a hand. "Maybe they can get prints." Vince, Raymond and she had already handled their notes. But Liv, and possibly Alex, hadn't.

Ray frowned. "Someone knows a lot about us."

"You know what's really creepy?" Vincent lowered his voice, his tone ominous. "A month ago, someone pretending to be Mona messaged me on Facebook, begging me to come here."

Ray's eyes widened. "Me, too."

Liv nodded and Amber sighed. "I think we all received the same messages."

Flashes of blue and red tugged her gaze to the shaded drive, where two emergency vehicles moved toward them.

Someone had lured them all here. Now they each had a piece of paper bearing a single line of print.

And one of them had died tonight. Whatever had happened to Alex, the notes tied the five of them together. Monday morning, she'd ask some questions.

First would be how did Ramona Freeborn die?

Caleb opened the door to the white RAV4 and watched Amber slide into the driver's seat. "Thanks for your help tonight."

She gave him a tired smile. "No problem. I figured you guys could use an extra body."

Yeah, they could have used two or three. But he and Amber, plus the four other law enforcement personnel who'd arrived, had managed to talk to everyone and get whatever information they could. Which wasn't much. No one had seen anyone go up or down the stairs, and no one had witnessed O'Dell fall.

Now, at a few minutes past eleven, the remaining guests were back inside, a shocked sense of loss overshadowing their earlier revelry. The body had been removed, but Crime Scene was still there, combing the area for evidence.

And he was officially on the clock. After four years with Levy County, he'd finally made his goal of being assigned to the Criminal Investigations Division. But being the low guy on the totem pole, he was stuck with the night shift. He was getting used to it. Strong coffee helped.

He pulled a pen and pad from his shirt pocket. He'd retrieved both from his glove box earlier. "I can reach you through Cedar Key, but how about giving me your cell number?" When he'd finished jotting it down, he scrawled his own number and tore the sheet from the pad. "Call me with any updates."

"I will. Please keep me in the loop."

"You're there whether you want to be or not. Though you and Ramona didn't keep in touch with the old gang, you were all pretty tight in high school. These notes tie you together again. Five of you, anyway."

She pulled her lower lip between her teeth. The soft glow of the parking lot light illuminated the concern in her eyes. She fastened the seat belt across her lap before tugging loose the blond locks trapped by the shoulder harness. Her dress rested a few inches above her knees, the fabric a shade his designer sister would call teal. Both the hem and the neckline were more modest than ninety percent of the attire he'd seen tonight. At least on the women. She apparently wasn't trying to draw male attention.

She'd gotten it, anyway, until she'd escaped to an empty table at the back of the room. She'd been pretty as long as he'd known her. In high school, he hadn't been interested. He'd stayed away from girls who were bad news. And Amber Kingston had been bad news in capital letters.

Now she was an upstanding citizen. But he still wasn't interested, for entirely different reasons.

"Be careful driving home." He stepped aside and closed her door.

As she moved away, her taillights disappeared into the trees lining the curved drive. A minute later he was in his vehicle, following the same path. He was a little overdressed in his suit, but his plans to cut out around ten and go home to change clothes hadn't materialized. Shedding the jacket would help.

He turned onto US 27 and released a sigh. It'd be easy to chalk up tonight's death to another drunk being careless. They didn't have O'Dell's blood alcohol levels yet, but according to several people, the guy hadn't taken it easy on the booze. People did stupid stuff when drunk. Things like sitting on balcony railings, tempting fate. Except based on the way O'Dell landed, he'd been facing outward when he began his plunge. Had he leaned too far over the railing and lost his balance?

But that didn't explain what he was doing up there to begin with. Everyone's testimony backed up what he remembered—O'Dell was gregarious and loud, not the type to seek out solitude. Which meant someone was lying about not being with him.

That wasn't all that was fishy. He didn't know about Alex, but the other former comrades in crime had all received Facebook messages from someone posing as Ramona, claiming to have cancer. Was that what had killed the real Ramona or had it been something more sinister?

By the time he reached the sheriff's office in Bronson fifteen minutes later, he'd come up with a dozen questions and zero answers. On his way to his office, he poked his head into a doorway.

"Learn anything yet?"

Detective Frank Mason shifted his gaze from the computer screen. "Alex O'Dell apparently kept his nose clean. Nothing on his record but a couple of speeding tickets. He's worked for Zanardi Construction since 2012. In the morning, we'll talk to his neighbors, friends and family members to see if he had any enemies."

"Have you checked out Ramona Freeborn yet?"

"Haven't had a chance." The desk chair squeaked as Mason shifted position. Built like a linebacker, his girth filled it. No one would mess with Frank Mason, even without the pistol at his side.

Caleb rested his palm on the doorjamb. "I'll see what I can find."

He moved down the hall toward his office. Amber had given him a middle name and date of birth. According to the fake Facebook profile, Ramona lived in Fort Lauderdale. That at least gave him a starting point.

He slid into the swivel chair and removed the notepad from his pocket. While waiting for his computer to boot up, he skimmed his notes, pausing to reread one line.

"The day is sunny and skies are blue." The words were from the paper Crime Scene had retrieved from Olivia Chamberlain's purse. If that was meant to describe Liv, the meaning was pretty obscure. Maybe she was naturally a cheerful person. He hadn't seen it tonight.

The message found near Alex made more sense. Sort of. "The kids all adore you, their referee." Alex was a coach, not a referee. Whoever had written it may have not known the difference.

He jumped to Vincent Mahoney's line before flipping the page back. "The day is sunny and skies are blue. All of life's pleasures surround you." Did the five lines form a poem?

He grabbed a legal pad and scrawled what he'd read. Two other lines rhymed. After writing the fifth, he scanned the page.

The day is sunny and skies are blue.
All of life's pleasures surround you.
Once you were bound, but now you're free.
The kids all adore you, their referee.
A sworn public servant, you've answered the call.

His brow creased. A line was missing, the final word rhyming with *call*. But no one else had received a note. He and other law enforcement had asked the question of everyone at the reunion.

He reached for the mouse. Ramona Freeborn. The sixth friend. Had she received a mysterious message, making up the last line of the poem? He leaned forward and, after a couple of clicks, started typing.

During the next several minutes he found two Ramona Freeborns, one much older and the other slightly younger. When a third one came up, his pulse quickened. The date of birth matched. And she'd lived in Fort Lauderdale. As he read, a lead weight settled in his gut.

Ramona Freeborn had been murdered.

Investigative records provided details. Her body had been found in the woods five miles from where she'd lived. She'd disappeared late in the evening from her home, where she resided alone, having been divorced for nine months. There'd been no sign of forced entry. She'd either known the killer or had stepped outside and been abducted.

He moved on to the evidence list. Nothing of significance had been found at the house. In the woods, about ten feet from the body, lay a bloody wooden baseball bat. He'd seen some gruesome things in the line of duty, but the pictures that followed sent bile surging up his throat. Someone had beat Ramona to a bloody pulp.

More reports came after the initial one. Interviews with neighbors who'd seen nothing. Statements from coworkers saying they couldn't imagine anyone wanting to hurt her. Even her ex had nothing negative to say, claiming their divorce had been amicable, a fact supported by several of her friends.

There was another piece of evidence—a sheet of paper, apparently carried by the wind and lodged in some underbrush outside the initial crime scene perimeter. As he read the words, a cold blanket of dread covered him.

The missing line of the poem.

He reached for the phone but hesitated. Amber would be asleep. But first thing tomorrow, he'd make the call. He had to warn her and her friends.

Because this final line changed everything.

TWO

Amber poured dry cat food into a large mixing bowl, the sound of kibbles hitting metal echoing through the house. Two gray streaks zipped into the kitchen, followed by a yellow tabby and a solid black cat. It didn't matter that they'd had their fill of moist food before she'd left for her morning run. Having spent too much of their lives perpetually hungry, they still acted as if each meal might be their last.

Except Tippy. She lay on the kitchen table, proud and regal, working on her after-breakfast bath. She resembled a chocolate point Siamese, but white tipped her feet, face and tail. A snowshoe, according to someone at Sheltering Hands, the Williston cat rescue. Amber had brought in pictures and gotten the official opinion shortly after Tippy had joined the Kingston household.

A ringtone interrupted her thoughts and she jogged into the living room, ponytail swishing against her neck. She retrieved her phone from the coffee table and frowned at the unfamiliar number before giving a tentative hello.

"Are you up?" It was Caleb.

"Just finished my morning run. I'm having breakfast then heading to Walmart in Chiefland."

"At seven thirty in the morning?"

She strolled into the kitchen and Tippy stopped midlick, ready for the petting she knew would be forthcoming. Amber had halfheartedly tried to train her but had given up. That was one of the joys of living alone. There was no one to tell her cats don't belong on the table. Or that five was too many.

"I have to be at work later this morning. But I've got friends coming for pizza and movies tonight, and my TV croaked."

"How about meeting me for breakfast?"

Was he asking her out? She eyed the green concoction waiting in the blender on the kitchen counter: her breakfast smoothie. "I've already got it made."

"Coffee then? We need to talk."

The seriousness in his tone killed the possibility the call was anything but professional. An irrational twinge of disappointment passed through her. "Is everything all right?"

"There are some things you need to know."

Her stomach tightened. "Where do you want to meet?"

"Huddle House in Chiefland."

"Give me forty minutes." Date or not, she wasn't meeting him in a ponytail and Spandex. After pouring her drink into a quart-size Mason jar, she hurried down the hall to change into a pair of jeans and a scoop-neck T-shirt. By the time she'd finished, the jar was empty.

When she arrived at Huddle House, Caleb was inside. She took a seat opposite him.

"I already ordered. I hope you don't mind. Since I came from the station, I haven't eaten."

The waitress approached with a plate of eggs, pancakes and hash browns and placed it in front of him. After bringing Amber a cup of steaming water and a tea bag, she left them alone.

Amber started the tea steeping. "What did you learn?"

"We don't have anything back from the lab yet, but I uncovered some disturbing things about Ramona Freeborn's death." Beneath the sandy-blond hair, his brows were drawn together, and concern had settled in his eyes.

She frowned. "I'm guessing Mona didn't have cancer."

"I don't know, but I can tell you that's not how she died."

A vise clamped down on her chest. "Murder?"

"She was taken into the woods and beaten to death with a baseball bat."

Amber cringed at the mental image his words evoked. "Any idea who did it or why?"

"No. The case is still unsolved. But the killer left a piece of paper."

The vise squeezed harder. "Like what the five of us received at the reunion."

He pulled a page from the manila folder lying on the table and handed it to her. "I've written out all the messages and put them together."

After a brief moment she snapped her gaze to his face. "It's a poem." She hadn't recognized it before. Of course, she hadn't seen half the lines.

Caleb took a bite of eggs before pointing with his fork. "Ramona's line is the last one."

She nodded and, as she silently read, something cold and dark settled over her.

The day is sunny and skies are blue.
All of life's pleasures surround you.
Once you were bound, but now you're free.
The kids all adore you, their referee.
A sworn public servant, you've answered the call.
But one by one, justice will find you all.

When she met Caleb's eyes, he was studying her. "Any idea why somebody wants you guys dead?"

She swirled the tea bag in the mug and watched the liquid darken. She had an idea. It just didn't make any sense.

Caleb's gaze bore into her.

Finally she released a long breath. "Logan Cleary has always blamed us for his brother's death."

"Why?"

"I don't know. We didn't have anything to do with it." Her hands tightened around her mug. "I invited him to join us. Then I got sick and Liv took me home." The words came out more defensive than she'd intended and she softened her tone. "Landon never showed. But Logan has always blamed me. I don't know whether he thinks we hurt Landon, but he holds me accountable for inviting him in the first place."

She held herself accountable, too. Had for the past ten years. She just tried not to think about it. That was one reason she'd severed ties with all her old friends.

She sighed. "But why act now? I mean, it's been ten years."

"Logan has spent most of that time in the Army, so he's been gone. He got out a few months ago."

Yeah, that was what she'd heard. She'd run into him during one of his leaves. His animosity toward her was as strong as it had been right after Landon's murder. And judging from the glares he'd given her at the reunion, it hadn't faded.

Caleb poured syrup over his pancakes, the eggs and hash browns now gone. "What can you tell me about Landon's last day alive?"

"Same thing I told the police ten years ago. It was Sunday, two days after graduation. He'd asked me out at the commencement ceremony, and we'd made plans for dinner and a movie Monday night. Sunday he texted me and asked what I was doing. I told him I was going out later and partying with friends."

"How late?"

"Late. After Mom and Dad went to bed." She didn't have to tell him she'd been sneaking out. He knew. She could see the condemnation in his eyes. Or maybe her guilt was putting the condemnation there. That was something else she avoided thinking about, how her bad choices had affected her parents, especially her father.

"So you slipped out of the house after they went to bed."

The words sounded even worse coming out

of Caleb's mouth. He'd probably never caused his parents a moment's grief.

"What happened then?"

"I climbed out my bedroom window and Liv picked me up down the street. We went to the woods where Mona and the guys were. Raymond had raided his dad's liquor cabinet, like always. I don't remember what we were drinking, but we all got pretty wasted."

"Then you got sick."

She nodded. That had been a regular occurrence, too, drinking till she'd made herself sick. But she hadn't touched the stuff since that night. First Landon's death, then her father's heart attack—two life-changing events in the span of a week had scared her straight.

"After Liv dropped me off, she went home. The guys and Ramona said they left shortly after we did. No one saw Landon."

"You didn't let him know you were no longer at the party?"

A wave of guilt crashed down on her. "I didn't think about it." Or maybe she had, somewhere between bouts of throwing up. But the thought hadn't stayed in her pickled brain long enough to act on it.

"Anything else you can tell me?"

She shook her head, trying to tamp down another pang of guilt. There was something else, but it wasn't connected to Landon's murder. Not technically. If she brought it up now, the police would think they had something to hide. And they didn't.

Caleb washed his last bite of pancake down with coffee. "Alex's death is suspicious, but with Ramona, there's no doubt. She was murdered. The last line of the poem proves it wasn't random. This is someone's warped idea of justice."

She nodded and Caleb continued. "Frank Mason's the lead detective on the case. He's bringing the others up to speed, cautioning them about the danger. I told him I'd talk to you. But I'd like to meet with all of you and see if you can come up with some possible suspects. Logan is the most obvious. But it could be someone who'd been close to Landon."

"I'll get hold of them." They'd all exchanged numbers before leaving the reunion.

The waitress brought the checks and he claimed both of them. After he'd finished paying, he walked her to her vehicle. "I guess you're off to Walmart."

"And you're headed to bed."

"Not yet. Church first. I teach a preteen Sunday school class."

After bidding him farewell, she climbed into

the driver's seat. He was going to church. To teach Sunday school. He hadn't become a preacher.

But he was still way out of her league.

Amber wheeled her cart into the midmorning sunshine, a large, flat box protruding from the top at an angle. She'd gone with a forty-inch. Anything bigger wouldn't have fit on the shelf in her entertainment center.

As she moved down the center lane, she glanced around, an uneasy caution tightening her shoulders. The same uneasiness had plagued her since her meeting with Caleb. Mona was dead, brutally murdered. Alex's death probably wasn't an accident, either. Based on the poem, the rest of them were all marked. The question was, "Who's next?"

She dragged in a shaky breath and pressed her key fob. Several spaces away, the lights on her RAV4 flashed and the security system beeped. Soon she'd be loaded up and locked safely inside. From now on, she wouldn't go anywhere without her weapon, whether on duty or not.

After sliding the box into the back of her vehicle, she straightened to shut the door. Her heart stuttered. Logan Cleary stood at the driver's-side front quarter panel, arms crossed.

"Hello, Amber." He pushed her name off

his tongue as if it were something distasteful, then moved toward her, blocking her path to the door.

Her pulse raced and moisture coated her palms. She squared her shoulders. Whether she was armed or not, he'd have to be stupid to try accosting her at Walmart in broad daylight.

"What do you want, Logan?"

"I want a lot of things. A filet mignon dinner. Tickets to the Super Bowl." He rested a shoulder against her vehicle. "Justice."

"I'm sorry about Landon, but I had nothing to do with that."

"You can't deny those texts."

"I invited him to hang out with us."

"You lured him there, and your friends beat him up. What happened? Did a dare go bad? Did he cross one of you?"

"Logan, go home, or I'll call for security." She'd tried to talk to him shortly after Landon was killed. But he hadn't wanted to hear it. Ten years later, he still wasn't listening.

He pushed himself away from her vehicle. "I'll leave you alone for now. But know this. What goes around comes around. Sometimes it takes a while, but eventually karma has her way." He pivoted to walk away. "Two down, four to go." Though his back was turned, the words reached her, chilling her all the way to the core.

"Is that a confession?"

He hesitated, stiffening. When he turned around, the tension was gone. The usual cockiness emanated from him. "There's nothing for me to confess. But someone's making sure you guys pay for what you did. I'm just waiting for it to happen."

She climbed into her SUV but didn't pull from the space. *Two down, four to go.* It hadn't taken Logan long to realize he'd said too much. Was he taking vengeance for his brother's death or was he waiting for someone else to do it, as he'd claimed?

She watched him cross the lot and get into a red pickup. After he drove away, she shifted her vehicle into Reverse. Landon's death had been tragic. Whatever he'd done, he hadn't deserved to die in the way he had. No doubt his murder had left a hole in the lives of those who loved him. A hole his twin brother would feel for the rest of his life. And she'd unwittingly played a part, however small.

The fact that she hadn't intended Landon harm didn't matter to Logan. He'd charged, tried and convicted her.

All over a few innocent texts.

* * *

Caleb approached the double glass doors leading into the Gathering Table, a file folder tucked under one arm. According to the text Amber had sent him, she was already inside, along with Vincent and Raymond. Olivia hadn't arrived yet.

He stepped into the popular restaurant and scanned the large room. It wasn't crowded. Midafternoon on a Monday, it was too late for the lunch crowd but too early for the dinner crowd.

Meeting for a meal wasn't the usual way he conducted interviews. But these weren't typical witnesses. They were former classmates, although more acquaintances than friends. He had a dual purpose in bringing them together: to reiterate what he'd learned about Ramona and the danger they were in, and to find out what they'd done to make themselves targets. The latter was more likely to happen in the relaxed setting of the restaurant than in an interrogation room at the station.

As he made his way toward a double table at one edge of the room, Amber held up a hand and waved. He claimed the empty chair next to her and she flashed him a friendly smile.

"You know Ray and Vince. This is Vince's wife, Jessica."

He extended a hand across the table. When Amber had called him to finalize plans for their meeting, she'd told him Vince's wife would be with him. It was probably for the best. She could be in as much danger as her husband.

The glass door swung open and Olivia stepped inside. She gave an enthusiastic wave before moving toward them, shoulders back and head high. But there was tension in her features and a stiffness in her gait. The stress was wearing on her already.

She plopped into the chair next to Raymond. "Sorry I'm late. I probably had the shortest drive of any of you, and I'm the last one here. Go figure."

They'd decided on Chiefland as the place to meet, not because Caleb lived there, but because it was the most centralized. Raymond lived thirty-five minutes south, in the small town of Inglis, and Liv was only fifteen minutes west in Bronson. Amber, of course, came from Cedar Key, also a thirty-five-minute drive.

Vincent Mahoney was the only one who'd moved away from Levy County permanently. But since he and his wife had met a customer in Chiefland earlier, the location had been convenient for them, also.

After bringing drinks, the waitress left with their order of appetizers to share.

Vincent grinned at Amber. "I was hoping for some peanut butter cookies, but they weren't on the menu."

"Celery smeared with peanut butter." Raymond gave Amber a teasing punch to the shoulder. "That makes a great snack, too."

Amber frowned, but there was humor in the gesture. "No one gets to watch me swell up and turn blotchy today. You'll have to find your entertainment elsewhere."

Vincent turned to his wife. "Amber has a terrible allergy to anything containing peanuts. Can't get anywhere near the stuff."

As they waited for their food to arrive, conversation turned serious. Caleb reached for the manila folder. "I assume someone from the sheriff's office has brought you all up to speed."

They each nodded and he continued. "Then you're aware Ramona Freeborn was murdered. Someone hauled her into the woods and took a baseball bat to her."

Olivia gasped and brought her hands to her mouth. Raymond and Vincent cringed. Someone had apparently left out that detail.

Vincent shook his head, frowning. "So was Alex murdered, too?"

"We don't have a definitive answer yet, but it's a possibility, especially in light of the messages you each received." He opened the folder and read the six lines. "Individually, they're meaningless. But when read as a whole, ending with Ramona's, the threat is obvious. Someone has targeted you, seeking vigilante justice. So far, it looks like he's been successful twice." He paused to look at each of them. Every face registered concern. Raymond's right leg bounced up and down, the movement radiating into his torso. A touch of wildness had crept into his eyes.

Caleb rested his forearms on the table, his fingers entwined. "Any idea who or why?"

Before anyone could answer, the waitress returned with their drinks.

Leaving his straw on the table, Raymond chugged several swallows of his Coke, then jabbed a hand through his stringy, dishwater-blond bangs. They fell right back onto his forehead. "This is about Landon Cleary." He clutched his glass so tightly his knuckles turned white. His other hand was splayed on the red-checked tablecloth.

Amber nodded. "That's what I think."

Raymond shook his head, the movement causing his hair to fall into his eyes. He didn't bother to sweep it aside. "Somebody knows what we did."

Vincent shot him a warning glare. "We didn't *do* anything. Amber invited him to hang with us. Someone beat him up and smashed his head in with a rock. We never saw him, so we couldn't have *done* anything."

Raymond let out a pent-up breath. "That's not what I meant. He was coming to hang with us, so I feel responsible." He released his Coke to rest his hand on the table. The cuticles were stained dark, signs he made his living as a mechanic. He still wore his uniform with its embroidered Speedy Lube Express patch over the left pocket. Although he appeared calmer now, holding the anxiety at bay seemed to be requiring some effort.

"He wasn't coming to hang with us," Vincent said. "He was coming to hang with Amber. And you don't see her beating herself up over it."

Caleb slanted a glance at her. The tight jaw and downcast eyes told him a lot. Vincent was wrong. Amber *had* beat herself up. Plenty of times. Apparently she still did.

A pang of sympathy shot through him, along with the desire to wipe away her pain. He shook off the latter. He couldn't fix everyone's woes. He'd had to accept that fact a long time ago. Life was messier than it had been in high school, the enemies to happiness much more tenacious than a few school bullies.

He shifted his gaze to the others. "If this *is* about Landon Cleary, any ideas as to who might have appointed himself executioner?"

"Only one," Raymond said. "Logan."

Vincent nodded. "He's always blamed us. If anyone's decided to take vengeance for Landon's death, it would be Logan."

"Why do you say that?" He and Amber had already discussed Logan, and she'd updated him on the confrontation yesterday, but he wanted to hear what the others had to say.

Raymond shrugged. "I've only seen him a few times in the past ten years. He always stares daggers at me, like he wants to hurt me. I try to avoid him."

"Same here," Vincent said. "I ran into him several times the summer after graduation. He was always spouting off about the six of us doing something to his brother. The end of the summer, I left for college. Then I settled in Gainesville, so I never saw him until this past weekend."

The waitress approached with platters of nachos, onion rings, mozzarella sticks and fried pickles, then placed a stack of plates on the table. When she left, they each took samples and Vincent continued.

"Several times during the reunion, I caught Logan glaring at me. He was talking to people, even did some dancing. But the whole time, his eyes were on one of us. It was creepy."

Caleb picked up a mozzarella stick and bit off the end. "Did he say anything to you?"

Vincent shook his head. "Didn't need to. The threat was loud and clear without him opening his mouth."

"That's how he was with me, too," Liv said. "He never spoke to me, but every time I looked at him, he was staring real mean-like."

Caleb nodded. "If he showed up at your house, would you open the door?"

"No way." Raymond didn't even hesitate. "I'd call the police."

Vincent agreed. "None of us would let him in."

"Apparently Ramona did. She disappeared from her home late at night. There was no sign of forced entry. So she must have opened the door for the killer, which means it was likely someone she knew and didn't feel threatened by."

Vincent frowned. "I can't imagine who."

"Was there anyone Logan and Landon were close to who might do something like this?"

"They were close to a lot of people." Vincent waved a hand. "I mean, they were both pretty popular. But close enough to take this kind of vengeance?"

Amber released a slow breath. "I can see making some threats, but someone's got to be pretty warped to do what they did to Ramona." A shudder shook her shoulders. "Maybe she opened the door for another reason and the killer was waiting. She could have remembered something she left in her car. Or maybe she had a cat and was letting it in or out."

Caleb dipped his head. "It's a possibility." Logan was the most likely suspect. Actually he was their only suspect. He'd better have someone who could place him far from Fort Lauderdale on that night in April.

"I had a run-in with Logan yesterday." Amber's tone was somber as she relayed everything she'd told him previously.

When she'd finished, Raymond flopped back in his chair. "See? I told you. It's Logan. I know it is."

"We'll be talking to him." Caleb looked around the table. "Regardless, keep your eyes open and report anything suspicious. I don't care how insignificant it seems. And don't open your door for anyone."

As the six of them polished off the appetizers, the conversation topics grew increasingly light. By the time they'd finished and paid their bills, Caleb had heard at least a dozen stories of long-ago pranks, some likely embellished.

Vincent pushed his chair away from the table. "The wife and I still have to stop by the office before we can call it a day, so we'll need to split."

When Liv stood, the napkin fell from her lap and she bent to pick it up.

"Cool tattoo," Amber said.

Caleb followed her gaze. Liv's tight-fitting tank had ridden up, exposing a two-inch stretch of skin above the waistband of her jeans. An inked blue-green line crossed itself to form a sort of sideways cause ribbon. One side continued down and around, wrapping a scripted *LC*. Two red and green hearts framed the elaborate design like bookends.

Olivia wiggled her hips then posed, showing off the artwork.

"So who's LC?" Raymond asked.

"Liv Chamberlain." She cast the words over her shoulder.

Vincent cocked a brow. "You have your own initials tattooed on your back?"

She turned around, grinning. "It's a hint in case I forget who I am."

Vincent laughed. "That's our Liv."

Caleb had to agree. He'd had a few classes with her and she'd always been a little on the ditsy side. As long as he'd known her, she'd struck him as someone who liked attention— flamboyant, loud and boisterous. Ten years later she still dressed to be noticed, from the ridiculously high black stilettos to the rhinestone-studded dress jeans to the spiky auburn hair with its purple highlights. The auburn wasn't any more natural than the purple. Actually, he wasn't sure what her natural color was. Even in high school, she'd dyed it, sometimes blond, sometimes red, sometimes jet-black.

She shrugged, still grinning. "You never know when it might come in handy."

Raymond gave her a playful slap. "Especially if you party the way you used to."

Olivia raised her hand in a fist pump. "If there's a girl who knows how to party, it's me."

Caleb watched her lead the way to the door, a spring in her step, at least as much as the five-inch heels would allow.

The day is sunny and skies are blue.

Liv's line of the poem. The outlook of someone who was perpetually cheerful.

With Liv, it was probably an act. Her eyes held an underlying sadness the false cheeriness didn't quite mask. What was at its root? A burden that grew heavier with every passing year? A secret slowly eating a hole in her heart?

Raymond knew. Something, anyway. He'd gotten agitated enough to almost let it slip. Then Vincent had stopped him.

Caleb stepped out the door into the steamy afternoon. He needed to speak with Raymond alone. But first he'd pore over all the investigative reports from Landon's murder. The next time he met with any of them, he'd be armed with every fact he could get his hands on. He'd force some answers.

Whatever happened ten years ago, there was probably plenty the six of them had never told the police.

Secrets two of them had taken to their graves.

THREE

Amber turned onto Airport Road and stepped hard on the gas, lights flashing and siren blaring. Usually her shift consisted of helping tourists with directions or taking the report of an occasional stolen cell phone. This one had the potential to be much more exciting.

Two minutes ago a call had come in. A woman in distress. Someone had heard screams coming from the woods near the airport.

Amber's cruiser screeched to a halt in front of the area described by the caller, a patch of woods just past where the road straightened to parallel the runway. She stepped from the car and drew her weapon. From deep within the pines and palmettos, a rustle sounded and her senses shot to full alert.

"Hello?"

Another rustle. A shiver went up her spine.

"Cedar Key Police. Do you need assistance?"

A soft breeze blew, whispering through the

trees. But over the murmur of the wind was movement, much more substantial.

She tightened her grip on her weapon and called again. "Hello?"

This time there was a response, a raspy whisper. "Help me."

Her heart thudded. The victim. She was alive but likely hurt. Amber stepped into the woods, unclipping her radio from her belt. "I need backup. And possibly medical assistance." Once Cedar Key Fire Rescue responded, they'd determine whether an ambulance needed to come from the mainland.

She crept deeper into the woods, watching and listening for movement. The woman needed help, but whoever had attacked her might be lurking nearby. Charging in recklessly could get her killed. "Keep talking so I can find you."

Silence met her words. Maybe the victim had lost consciousness.

Or maybe there was no victim. Maybe the call was a hoax. She stopped walking and turned in a slow circle, pistol raised. A bead of perspiration traced a downward path between her shoulder blades. The sense of being watched was too strong to ignore. But except for the soft, steady rustle of the breeze through the trees, the woods were quiet.

Sirens sounded in the distance. They drew

closer then stopped, dying in quick succession. Backup had arrived, along with fire rescue.

"Amber?"

It was her brother Hunter's voice. Her breath escaped in a rush. "In here."

Moments later Hunter joined her, along with fireman and EMT Wade Tanner.

Hunter looked around them. "What have we got?"

"Right now? Absolutely nothing."

At their raised brows, she continued. "When I arrived, someone was in the woods. I heard rustling and a woman's faint cry. 'Help me.'"

At least she'd assumed it was a woman. Now she wasn't sure. The hoarse whisper could have belonged to anyone.

They spread out to comb the woods. When Hunter approached her a few minutes later, he was holding a fillet knife wrapped in a handkerchief likely pulled from his pocket. A shudder rippled through her. That eight-inch blade could have done some serious damage. Had someone planned to use it on her but was scared off when the others arrived?

Hunter indicated what he held. "I found this on the ground. Since the water's pretty close, it's possible a fisherman dropped it. We'll see if we can lift prints, anyway."

Over the next half hour, the three of them

knocked on doors and searched the long, narrow stretch of land housing the Cedar Key Airport. They came up with nothing, other than the knife. Wade opened the driver's door of the Ford rescue vehicle. At least he hadn't brought the ladder truck to this wild-goose chase.

She flashed him an apologetic smile. "Sorry I brought you out here for nothing. When I heard someone call for help, I was afraid we might need you."

"No problem. It added some excitement to my afternoon. You think it was kids playing around?"

"Maybe." That scenario was better than the one she'd come up with.

He shut the door and Hunter stepped up beside her. "Do you really believe that?"

Wade cranked the engine and pulled onto the road, leaving her alone with Hunter.

"Honestly? No." She walked toward her car. This wasn't going to turn out well. Hunter had that big-brother's-gonna-protect-his-little-sister look in his eye. As soon as he'd learned there'd been a suspicious death at her reunion, he'd contacted Levy County to get details. Then he'd bombarded her with questions.

His footsteps pounded behind her. "You shouldn't respond to calls like this alone."

She spun and planted her hands on her hips.

"How long do you think Chief Sandlin's going to keep me if I can't do my job?" After a year as a part-time officer, supplementing her pay with waitressing, she'd recently made full-time. She wasn't about to jeopardize it.

Hunter stared her down, jaw tight. "How well do you think you'll do your job if you're dead?"

She jerked open the cruiser door. Hunter needed to mind his own business. She'd lived under his shadow her whole life.

Through her teen years he'd tried to keep her out of trouble. It hadn't worked. She'd resented what she'd perceived as his holier-than-thou attitude and bossy ways. Unable to measure up, she hadn't even tried. It had been easier to follow in Harold's downhill footsteps than to climb the path Hunter trod.

Ten years later everything had changed, yet nothing had. She was a responsible adult, living an upstanding life, and Hunter was still telling her what to do.

"Come on, Amber." He wasn't yelling but his voice was raised beyond its usual mellow tone. "This guy has already killed two people. You're on the list."

"I'm armed."

"It won't matter if he takes you out from behind."

She slid into the seat and gripped the wheel.

Whatever had made her think she could work alongside her older brother without him trying to micromanage her life?

Hunter lowered his voice. "I'm not trying to control you. I just don't want you taking unnecessary chances. Most of what we do is pretty safe. But if you get any weird calls, respond with backup."

She released her grip on the wheel. He was right. Someone had tried to get her alone and she'd almost played into his hands. Those last moments before Hunter and Wade arrived, she'd been scared. Whoever was after her and the others wasn't going to stop until he was caught. Or they were all dead.

"All right." She heaved a sigh. "If I'm not driving around town, answering touristy questions and keeping people from speeding, I'll make sure I'm with someone."

Hunter's mouth curved into a relieved smile. "Thank you. I'll breathe much easier."

She closed the door and watched him walk to the SUV. He only got into her business because he loved her. And she loved him, although he annoyed her sometimes.

She started the car and made her way toward downtown. Her shift would soon be over. She'd go by the station, write up her report then head for home.

When she pulled into her driveway thirty minutes later, three of her cats were sitting in the front windows, having weaved in behind the vertical blind slats. Tippy occupied a windowsill by herself. Smokey and Ash, the gray sisters, shared the second. Cimba and Shadow were likely sleeping on the couch.

Of the five, only Tippy was hers. The other four were visitors, cats she was fostering for Sheltering Hands. Over the past several months, a dozen others had passed through her place on their way to forever homes.

She retrieved her purse from the passenger seat and her gaze slid across the lower right-hand corner of the windshield. Something white was tucked under the tip of the wiper blade.

As she stepped from the vehicle, dread trickled over her. No one seemed to be watching, but she couldn't be sure. Woods lined Hodges Avenue and most of the streets running off it— 165th Terrace was no exception. Maybe she should have rented something a little more open.

She moved to the back of the RAV4 to retrieve a pair of latex gloves. What lay jammed beneath the wiper blade wasn't an advertisement or note from someone she knew. It had been placed too inconspicuously. It was folded in eighths, its size and location almost guaranteeing she'd be the one to discover it. In fact, she'd almost missed it herself.

After donning the gloves, she pulled the paper from the glass and took it inside the house.

Block print filled the page. Six lines. As she read what she held, her blood turned to ice.

She laid the sheet on the table and took her phone from her purse. She could call Caleb directly and leave Hunter out of it. No, Caleb was probably asleep, getting his rest before going in to work all night. She needed to go through the proper channels, which meant reporting it to her own police department.

When she opened the door several minutes later, Hunter frowned at her. "What's going on?"

"Come in and I'll show you." She led him to the table and pointed to the sheet of paper. "Someone slipped this under my wiper blade at the station."

As he read, she followed along.

One by one, the days tick by.
One by one, the moments fly.
One by one, plans are set.
One by one, goals are met.
One by one, mistakes are made.
And one by one, debts are paid.

Hunter's eyes met hers. He was still frowning. "What do you think it means?"

"Like the other poem, it's referencing our successes."

"And the mistakes?"

"Ramona's mistake was opening the door. For Alex, it was venturing up on that balcony."

"And with each death, a debt was paid."

Her gaze dipped to the page. "I wonder if the others got this."

"If not, I'm even more concerned."

Her eyes again locked with his. "Why?"

"It might mean you're next."

Caleb dried his plate and put it in the cupboard. Voices drifted to him from the living room, an evening sitcom he had no intention of watching. But conversation, no matter how senseless, made the house feel less lonely.

He closed the cabinet door and left the kitchen. He'd finished dinner. Or maybe it would be breakfast, since he'd gotten up only two hours ago. When most of the eastern US was getting ready for bed, his day was just starting. Eventually he'd put in for days. But after several weeks, he was pretty used to the backward schedule.

When he came into the living room, a set of green eyes and a pair of dark brown ones followed him. He walked toward the recliner and excitement rippled along the dog's back. Rescued a year ago, Kira was a beagle mix who loved cuddling, chasing squirrels and eating, in that order. As soon as his body met the leather surface, the dog landed in his lap with a *whoomph*.

He laughed and scratched her neck. "Good thing you're not a Saint Bernard or I'd be in trouble."

Not willing to share a lap with a dog, Tess jumped onto the arm of the recliner and began to purr. Caleb slid his fingers through her silky gray fur before reaching for the remote. As usual, he'd brought work home. One file sat on the kitchen table, still open from where he'd been reading it at dinnertime. The other was on the end table next to him. Sometimes things that eluded him at the station came to him in the comfort of his home. Reviewing work also made a great way to pass the evening.

He lowered the volume on the TV and laid down the remote. But instead of reaching for the file, he shifted his weight under Kira's white, tan and black body to pull his cell phone from its pouch. He didn't have anything new to tell Amber. When he'd gone in last night, he'd relayed what she and her friends had told him about Logan. Someone would make contact with him today.

Caleb had also printed the investigative reports connected with Landon Cleary's murder. Nothing had jumped out at him. Amber and her friends had given statements. Each person's story confirmed the others'. One hundred percent. Either they were all telling the truth or they'd coordinated everything before giving their statements to police. Caleb's gut told him it was the latter. Something was fishy. Raymond's actions at the Gathering Table had confirmed it.

Caleb had phoned him last night. Judging from the man's slurred speech, the call had caught him well into his evening binge. That should have worked in Caleb's favor. But Raymond had stuck by the same line he'd given after Vincent's warning glare. The booze hadn't loosened his tongue at all. He obviously functioned well while drunk.

Caleb brought up his contacts and scrolled to where Amber Kingston was listed first. After their meeting yesterday, he'd finally programmed her number into his phone. She was his main contact, the one most likely to tell him what he wanted to know. She was directly involved and had an inside link with the others.

And she was fellow law enforcement. It made sense to stay in close touch with her.

As he pressed the call icon, his pulse picked up a notch. Okay, he'd be lying if he didn't admit it. He was keeping in touch with her for all the professional reasons, but she intrigued him, too. Former bad girl turned cop. Expressive green eyes that revealed her emotions but shielded her secrets. An air that radiated confidence but a sense of regret that ran beneath the surface.

She answered with a "Hi, Caleb" instead of a generic hello. Maybe she'd programmed him into her phone, too.

Kira shifted in his lap. "You still awake?"

"For about another twenty minutes. What are you up to?"

"Sitting in my recliner buried under twenty-five pounds of canine sweetness."

"Aww. I like dogs, but I'm more of a cat person."

"I have one of those, too."

"I have…more than one." She paused. "Do they get along, your dog and cat?"

"I don't know if *get along* is the right way to describe it. They tolerate one another. I already had Tess, my cat, when I rescued Kira, so Kira's cool with cats. She just doesn't like other dogs. But I think Tess still hasn't fully forgiven me."

"She'll get over it. Eventually. Cats can hold a grudge for a long time."

"That's what I was afraid of." He stroked Tess's back and she stretched, front paws working in a kneading motion. "Have you talked to anyone since our meeting yesterday afternoon?"

"Liv called."

"What did she say?"

"She was scared. She wanted to know what I was doing to stay safe. I told her I'm being careful, keeping my eyes and ears open and my door locked, trying not to go out alone at night. Sleeping with my gun. Liv said she doesn't have one anymore."

"Liv had a gun?"

"In high school she had a rifle. She took lessons and competed. She was pretty good. Won a lot of ribbons. Used to regularly beat out the boys."

It was hard to picture Liv focused enough to be that competitive. "Maybe she should consider getting one again." He switched the phone to his other ear. "Did you talk to anyone else?"

"Nope, just Liv."

"I don't have anything new to add, either. I did learn the FBI is getting involved. With those notes tying you six together, and the obvious threat in Ramona's, everyone's treating these as serial killings."

"That's probably good. The more people looking at this, the better."

Kira stood to change her position. After rotating a quarter turn, she plopped down, her back against his belly, and he once again appreciated her smaller size. He ran a hand along her side and she released a contented sigh. "How was work today?"

"Interesting."

"Since Cedar Key isn't a hot spot for crime, I take it something out of the ordinary happened."

"I responded to a call, a woman screaming for help. When I arrived, I heard movement in the woods. Someone even said 'help me.' But whoever it was, never showed."

His chest tightened. "Do you think it was a hoax, a way to lure you into the woods alone?"

"It's pretty suspicious. First, whoever called said they wanted to remain anonymous. Nothing came up for the number, either. Probably a disposable cell. On the 911 recording, the voice was too raspy to even tell whether it was a man or woman."

She drew in a deep breath and released it in a sigh. "There are a few houses in the area. No one reported hearing screams. When I left the station, someone had put a note on my windshield."

"What kind of note?"

"A poem, six lines, the same rhyme pattern as the other one. Each line started with 'one by one,' ending with 'And one by one, debts are paid.'"

He swallowed hard. His stomach had twisted into a knot. "You need to be extra careful."

"I am. When I heard someone in the woods, I called for backup right away."

He finished the thought for her. "And went in without waiting for them to get there."

He couldn't blame her. He'd have done the same thing. When someone was in trouble, he jumped in with both feet. Had all his life.

She didn't respond and he continued. "You probably shouldn't handle any calls like that alone."

"You been talking to Hunter?" She gave a wry laugh. "He works for Cedar Key, too, and insists on playing the part of protective big brother."

Caleb smiled. Hunter had been five years ahead of them in school, but Caleb remembered him from the neighborhood. "In this case, you should probably listen." He paused briefly. "Any idea what Raymond was going to say before Vincent shut him up?"

"You noticed that, too." She sighed. "No idea. If any of them laid a hand on Landon, they've never breathed a word of it. Liv was with me, and everyone else has maintained that they left before Landon got there. I've never had reason to doubt them. We weren't the best kids, but we weren't killers."

The sincerity in her tone resonated with something deep inside him. She was telling the truth. Whatever happened, she hadn't been a part of it. An unexpected lightness filled his chest.

But the others had apparently kept something from her. They might not be capable of murder, but what about a prank gone wrong?

"If anyone hints otherwise, will you let me know?"

"Of course."

Caleb glanced at his watch. "I've got to take Kira out before I leave. I always keep her on a leash. The squirrels in the neighborhood thank me."

Amber laughed. "I hope I get to meet her sometime."

Not gonna happen. It wasn't like he'd be inviting her over for pizza and movies. The only women who visited his personal space were his sister and his mother. He didn't believe in setting up impossible expectations.

After disconnecting the call, he removed a reluctant dog from his lap. Tess relinquished her place on the padded arm and jumped down, rather than waiting for him to disturb her. They were great company, but intelligent conversation was lacking. Though the TV dispelled the silence, it never quite chased away the loneliness.

Eventually he'd be ready to risk his heart again. But when the time came, it would be with someone he could keep safe, not a woman whose job put her in potential danger every day. The world was a nasty place. He'd experienced the worst it had to offer firsthand.

When he arrived at the station, he got caught up on everything that had transpired since he'd ended his shift the prior night. Logan Cleary had an alibi for the night Ramona Freeborn was killed, an ex-girlfriend he'd spent the weekend with. A *married* ex-girlfriend whose husband had been out of town. Since Danielle had a whole lot to lose if her indiscretion was made public, he was inclined to believe her.

So if Logan was behind the killings, he wasn't working alone. Who would be willing to take up his vendetta? Someone who cared a lot for him. Likely someone they all knew.

Caleb sat in his office chair and pulled out the reports he'd printed last night. The time of death was set between 1:00 and 2:00 a.m. Someone had used the boy as a punching bag, then struck him in the head with a rock. Said rock was lying nearby, along with some others scattered around. The medical examiner had ruled out the possibility Landon had been running and had fallen. Otherwise he'd have thrust his hands out in front of him, leaving scrapes and debris. But his palms had been clean. His knees, too.

Although the cause of death was clear, they'd never been able to nail down the perpetrators. The boys and Ramona had said they'd left the woods at around twelve thirty. Amber and Liv had left thirty minutes earlier.

Raymond's parents had said he had a 1:00 a.m. curfew and had made it home with time to spare. Vincent and Alex had met a friend at Strickland Park, all three boys' statements putting them there well before one. Liv claimed to have gone home after dropping Amber off but had no one to corroborate her story. Ramona hadn't, either. She'd supposedly sneaked back into her house at twelve forty-five without disturbing anyone.

Amber hadn't been so lucky. While climbing in her bedroom window, she'd slipped and sent a lamp crashing to the floor. According to the statement her parents gave, this had happened shortly after midnight. From everything he knew about them, they were probably telling the truth. He wasn't sure about Alex and Vincent's friend, though.

He pulled up the transcript of his statement. The friend's name was Steve Wilkins, likely in the same graduating class as the others, according to his date of birth. When Caleb ran his information through the database, several pages of arrests came up. The guy had been in trouble from the time he'd graduated until about two years ago, which made him a pretty shaky witness for Alex and Vincent.

So that left only Amber and Raymond with airtight alibis. He pulled two statements from underneath the stack and laid them on top of Wilkins's. Theodore and Donna Ellis. He had no reason to doubt Raymond's parents' words, but typed their names into the search field anyway. They were both clean.

He rubbed his chin with a thumb and forefinger. What were the four of them hiding? What would Raymond have spilled if Vincent's subtle warning hadn't shut him up?

He entered Raymond's name. Besides the

Georgia drug charge he'd done time for, he had a couple of DUIs and a Trespassing. That was all.

Was there someone Raymond may have talked to, someone outside their group? A close friend? A family member?

He had an older brother who'd been two years ahead of them in school. What was his name? Ronald. He'd gone by Ron. On a whim, Caleb typed in Ronald Ellis's name, then scrolled through the lengthy record. His charges began shortly after he'd turned eighteen—two that year, three the following year... Caleb's gaze snapped back to one of the dates. June 3. Landon Cleary's date of death. It couldn't have been related. There'd been no arrests made in connection with Cleary's death.

Caleb clicked to pull up the record. Possession. He'd been stopped at 1:46 a.m. due to a nonfunctioning tag light. After finding crack cocaine in the console, the officer had arrested Ronald and had him booked into Levy County Detention. A passenger had been released.

A passenger by the name of Raymond Ellis.

Caleb looked at the time of arrest again, then picked up Theodore Ellis's statement. Ronald had been stopped at 1:46 a.m. Raymond had been with him.

But Raymond's parents had stated he was home before one.

Raymond's parents had lied.

FOUR

Amber moved down the hall at a good clip, purse slung over her shoulder. She was leaving the station late. She'd finished a report about a lost tablet five minutes after the official end of her shift then stopped by Chief Sandlin's office to tell him about the dangers she was facing. Hunter had already beaten her to it. She'd scold her meddling big brother later. At least she still had a job.

Actually her chief had been more concerned about the threats on her life than any inability to handle her duties. He'd agreed with Hunter that she shouldn't report alone to any out-of-the-ordinary calls. The other ninety-nine percent of her job, she could easily and safely do. Hunter was right about one thing. When it came to Florida cities, Cedar Key was one of the safest.

She swung open the glass door and stepped into the department's gravel parking area. A dark blue pickup sat next to her SUV, its engine running. Caleb was inside. He'd texted her earlier, asking if he could meet with her. He hadn't said what was so important that it warranted an in-person visit instead of a phone call.

He turned off the engine and lowered the window. "Howdy, stranger."

"Hey, yourself. Sorry you had to wait on me."

He gave her an easy smile. "No problem."

No problem for him, maybe, but it was putting stress on her already tight schedule. She would let Caleb talk to her while they shared leftover lasagna. At six thirty, she'd boot him out the door and head for her seven o'clock appointment.

She pressed the key fob and motioned with her other hand. "Follow me."

Seven minutes later she pulled into her driveway, Caleb behind her. Three cats were pressed together on one windowsill, Tippy on the other.

"You have four cats."

"Five."

"The proverbial cat lady." His tone was teasing.

"Almost." She inserted her key into the lock and turned it. "Actually, I only have one cat. The other four are foster cats."

"Foster cats?"

She swung open the door. "I'm a volunteer

for Sheltering Hands, a cat rescue over in Williston. I take care of them until they get placed in forever homes."

As she gathered empty bowls and put them in the sink to soak, cats wove in and out of her legs, emitting a chorus of meows.

Caleb smiled. "I wouldn't have pegged you as someone who'd be taking care of a bunch of homeless cats. But I wouldn't have pegged you as someone who'd have become a cop, either."

Yeah, it'd probably be a while before Caleb could look at her and not see the troubled rebel of ten years ago. Maybe that impression would never die.

She cleaned the dishes and lined the five of them up on the counter. When she popped the top on a large can, the protests grew louder.

"Trust me, you're not going to starve before I get this dished up."

Caleb laughed. "You won't convince them. I've got a cat and a dog that haven't missed a meal since they've been with me. But they're sure I'll let them go hungry sooner or later."

When she'd split the can between the five bowls, she picked up two of them and Caleb followed with the other three. Moments later, all five cats were lined up against the wall, smacking happily.

Amber pulled a casserole dish from the refrigerator and filled two plates. "Everything's going to be fast and easy tonight." She was even skipping the salad, a rare occurrence. She usually tried to eat fairly healthy. Too many depended on her, both people and animals.

Caleb carried one plate to the microwave. "I'm not hard to please. Anything's fine if I don't have to cook it."

Soon the mouthwatering aromas of Italian cooking filled her kitchen. She was feeding him leftovers, but they were good ones. She'd made the lasagna fresh last night.

The microwave beeped for the second time, and she set both steaming plates on the table next to the tea glasses she'd already placed there. After claiming an empty chair, she picked up her fork and cut into the steaming lasagna.

"So tell me what's so important—" Her gaze fell on Caleb's bowed head. "Sorry."

She knew better. She'd been raised the same way Caleb had. With him it had stuck. With her it hadn't. It wasn't that she no longer believed in God. She just wasn't going to pretend to be something she wasn't.

He lifted his head and opened his eyes. "What's so important that I wanted to talk to you in person?"

"Yeah."

He gave her a smile. When Caleb smiled,

the gesture projected more than simple friend-
liness. It held respect, even acceptance. For a
brief moment she could almost believe she
stood on equal ground with him.

"Last night, I was reviewing the reports from
Landon's murder investigation. I decided to do
some checking on the witnesses, particularly
those who provided alibis for each of you during the time Landon was killed."

As Caleb talked, her chest clenched. The
people who'd placed her home by midnight
were her parents. They'd been through enough.
They didn't need to be dragged back into a
murder investigation, their integrity doubted.
"You checked out my mom and dad?"

"I didn't feel the need. From everything I
knew about them, the likelihood of them giving a false statement, even to protect you, was
slim. So I started with Steve Wilkins."

She nodded, the tension dispelling only
slightly. She didn't like where the conversation
was headed. Caleb must have learned something incriminating or he wouldn't be sitting at
her kitchen table eating leftover lasagna.

"Alex and Vincent supposedly met him at
Strickland Park well before one, and they all
hung out there for a couple of hours before
going home." He cut off a bite-size piece and
brought it to his mouth. After a short pause

he continued. "Steve's been in and out of jail several times over the past ten years. Not the most upstanding citizen to provide a believable alibi."

Relief trickled over her. So he wasn't the most honorable guy around. It didn't mean he'd lied about meeting the others.

"After that, I checked out Raymond's parents."

There was more. She should have known.

"They were both clean. Then I looked up the criminal history on Raymond's brother Ronald."

She drew her brows together. What did Ronald have to do with it? "Ronald was older than all of us. Other than him sometimes giving Raymond a ride, we never saw much of him."

Caleb shrugged. "I didn't think I'd find anything, either. It was a long shot. Turns out he's had several arrests, one of which was on the night Landon was killed."

She frowned. "What was he arrested for?" If Ronald had been detained in connection with Landon's death, she'd have heard something, if not from the police, from Raymond and the others.

"He was stopped for a nonfunctioning tag light. It was the crack cocaine sitting in the console that sent him to jail."

She shook her head. "I still don't see what that has to do with Landon's murder."

"He had a passenger with him."

The pieces fell into place and she released a pent-up breath. "Raymond."

He nodded. "They were stopped at 1:46 a.m. Raymond's parents said he was home well before one."

"They lied." A blanket of dread wrapped around her and the few bites she'd eaten congealed into a doughy lump. Had Raymond's parents lied for him to keep him from taking the rap for something he hadn't done? Or to help him cover up something he *had* done? Had her friends gone through with the vengeance they'd threatened?

Amber dipped her gaze to where two-thirds of her meal sat untouched. She poked at a small piece she'd cut off, then pushed it across her plate. Her appetite had vanished.

Caleb picked up his tea and swirled the ice around in the glass. "I've had a gut feeling there's more to this than what was told to police." His gaze held hers. "I'm sure Raymond's parents aren't the only ones who lied about that night."

His implied accusations, coupled with her own guilt, twisted her insides into a knot. "I did not lie." She enunciated each word, her tone cold. "My only involvement was sending Landon the texts. If my friends hurt him, I don't know anything about it. I wasn't there. And they haven't told me anything."

He continued to eat but his eyes remained locked on hers. As he stared her down, she fought the urge to squirm.

Finally he laid down his fork and entwined his fingers, elbows resting on the table. "Amber, I need you to tell me everything, even if it seems unrelated."

Yeah, she had information that was unrelated. At least she'd thought it was. But knowing her friends had lied to the police changed everything.

She drew in a deep breath. Liv had begged her not to tell anyone. And Amber had given in to her request. She'd been wrong. Regardless of the promises she'd made ten years earlier, it was time to break her silence.

"Landon raped Liv." As she said the words, another shot of guilt stabbed her. Had her silence kept justice from being done? Worse yet, had it led to Mona's and Alex's deaths?

"When?"

"A couple of weeks before he was killed."

Caleb nodded. "How did you find out?"

"Liv told me. She told all of us."

"Tell me how this conversation came about."

"It was the night Landon was killed. We were at our hangout in the woods. I told everybody Landon and I were going to start dating and I'd invited him to party with us. Liv got really agitated. She jumped up, then whirled on me and asked how I could do that to her. I asked her why she didn't want me dating Landon. That's when she told us."

"That he raped her?"

She nodded. "They'd gone out to dinner. Afterward he pulled over on a deserted stretch of 19. They were making out. I guess things were progressing farther or faster than she wanted. When she tried to stop him he forced himself on her." Amber suppressed an involuntary shudder. That could have been her.

"What did you do then?"

"We were upset. We told her she needed to report it to the police."

"Did she?"

"No. She didn't want anybody to know. We told her that Landon needed to pay for what he'd done."

Caleb gave a knowing nod and she lifted a hand.

"That's not what I meant. We wanted him to pay with jail time, not his life. But we couldn't talk her into making a report. Landon's dad was a criminal defense lawyer. He had money and a lot of connections. Liv was sure her name would be dragged through the mud and Landon would go free."

"What happened then?"

"One of the guys said they should take it out of his hide. The others joined in, talking about how they were going to teach him a lesson, that when they got through with him, he wouldn't even look at another girl."

"What were they talking about doing to him?"

"Beating him up."

"Did you think they were really going to do it?"

She shook her head. "By then we'd all had a lot to drink. You know how guys get when they're drunk. They talk tough, but it's a lot of hot air."

"What else was said?"

"That was it. The rest of the night was our usual stuff. Then I got sick and Liv took me home."

"When did you hear from any of them again?"

"The next day. Liv called to tell me Landon had been killed. They'd found his body in the woods. I asked her if the guys had done it. I knew they wouldn't have killed him intentionally, but I thought maybe they got carried away. Liv said it wasn't them, that they'd left shortly after we did, before Landon showed up. I talked to Mona and each of the guys after that, and they told me the same thing."

"You believed them?"

She shrugged. "I didn't have any reason not to. These people were my friends. We trusted each other."

Or the rest of them had trusted each other. Apparently they hadn't trusted her. The realization left her with an odd mix of emotions—hurt over being excluded and relief that she'd been spared the decision of whether or not to betray her friends.

"That's everything I know, including the things I didn't think were relevant." She stabbed the bite of lasagna she'd been pushing around the plate and put it in her mouth. Ever since learning of Mona's murder, the secret she'd carried had grown increasingly heavy, even more so since Ray's near slip at the Gathering Table.

She gave Caleb a half smile. "You wanted to meet with me in person instead of over the phone, hoping you'd be able to tell if I was hiding something."

"Busted." He flashed her a crooked grin and her stomach made a funny little flip.

"So did I pass the test?"

"I believe you, if that's what you're asking."

"Good." That was important, for more reasons than his position as a law enforcement officer. What he thought of her mattered on a personal level, too.

Caleb picked up his fork and resumed eating. "Why didn't you tell the police about Landon raping Liv?"

His tone was matter-of-fact but accusation had crept back into his eyes.

"We'd all promised Liv we wouldn't tell anyone. Besides, I didn't think it was related."

"Your friends talked about teaching Landon a lesson and a few hours later he's found dead near your hangout in the woods. You didn't think that might be an important thing to mention?"

"Look, I was seventeen. I made a mistake. I'm sure you've never made a bad decision in your life because you're perfect." Always had been. During junior high and high school, she'd gotten wind of a couple of fights he'd been in, intervening when a school bully was picking on a smaller kid. Even his "wrongs" were admirable.

She rose from the table and strode toward the sink. Half of her dinner still sat on her plate, but it had become as appealing as a bowl of earthworms.

When she reached the sink, she squirted some dish soap into the empty casserole dish.

The soft scrape of Caleb's chair against the tile warned her he'd risen from the table, but when he laid a hand on her shoulder, she started.

"Hey, it was just a question."

Yeah, it was a question—with judgment behind it.

She'd asked him if she'd passed the test. He hadn't answered directly. He'd simply told her he believed her.

That was because she *didn't* pass the test. With Caleb, she never would.

No matter what she did or who she helped, the stain left by her past would never fade.

Caleb laid his tackle box and pole in the bed of the Ford, ready to head for one of his favorite fishing spots—the pier at Cedar Key. He'd already made his early-morning trip to the gym. But before hitting the pier, he had an apology to make.

He climbed into the cab and pulled up the call log on his cell phone. *Lord, please help me make this right.*

When he'd left Amber's last night, an uneasy tension had hung between them. The last thing he'd wanted was to make her feel inferior. And he certainly hadn't wanted to heap more guilt on top of what she already experienced. Lord knew, he was well-acquainted with the emotion. He'd carried his own burden for the past four years.

He'd just been surprised, caught off guard. How could she think that information was irrelevant?

As a seventeen-year-old girl, maybe. Even not dredging it up in the intervening years made some sense. But she should've said something the night Alex died. Or at least the day they'd all convened at the Gathering Table.

In a sense, he understood. The longer one kept a secret, the harder it was to come clean. But Amber knew better. She was a cop.

He pressed the phone icon next to her name. Four rings later, she answered.

"Did I wake you up?"

"No. I was feeding the cats."

The tension he'd felt last night came through in her tone. In the background, a chorus of meows accompanied her words.

"I'm headed your way for some fishing. If you're not busy I'd like you to join me for breakfast. My treat."

"I've got things to do." The stiffness was still there, along with a lot of hesitation.

"You have to eat anyway, right?" When she didn't respond, he added, "I upset you last night and I'm sorry. Give me a chance to make it up to you."

Silence stretched between them. Finally she sighed. "All right. How about Annie's?"

"Sounds good." He hadn't eaten there but he'd passed it plenty of times coming into Cedar Key. He disconnected the call and slid the phone into the pouch at his hip.

When he pulled into the parking lot of Annie's, Amber was walking into the building.

A minute later he joined her at a table. "Thanks for meeting me. This gives me the opportunity to apologize in person."

She gave him a half smile. "Maybe I was a tad bit touchy."

"You're entitled. What you're dealing with would take a toll on anyone."

A waitress approached with some menus and took their drink orders. Once she left, he sat back in his chair. "How was your hot date?"

"I didn't say *date*. I said *appointment*."

"I'm good at reading between the lines. It's my job."

She grinned. "You're fishing."

"Maybe I am. Just curious. You know, trying to catch up."

Okay, maybe it was a little more than that. He *did* want to know her better. Something about her tugged at him. It was the sadness in her eyes, the tormented soul he sensed behind her tough exterior. She needed a friend, someone who understood what she was going through, the battles she'd fought alone for the past ten years. Friendship he could do.

"Okay, you're right." She rested her elbows on the table and interlaced her fingers. "I spent the evening with a man. I love him. He's kind and gentle and sweet."

As she spoke he refused to analyze the disappointment settling in his chest. So what if she was in a serious relationship? It wouldn't affect his interactions with her. Unless her guy was one of those jealous, possessive types.

Her eyes sparked with humor. "He's also eighty-seven."

At his raised brows she continued. "I'm a volunteer for Haven Hospice. Every couple of weeks I go sit with Mr. Danforth to give his wife a break. Tuesday night, she had a late dinner with friends."

He shook his head. The more he learned about Amber, the more she intrigued him. "I have to admit, the idea of you comforting terminally ill people is even less expected than your fostering homeless cats."

"I'm full of surprises."

And she was quickly earning his admiration and respect. "How long have you worked with Haven Hospice?"

"A couple of years. I visit the center regu-

larly and sit in people's homes several times a
month to give the caregivers a break."

"You work full-time, foster a bunch of cats
and volunteer for hospice. When do you take
time for yourself?"

She shrugged. "I like to stay busy."

"Busy is good. It's also a good way to burn
yourself out."

There was likely more behind her frenzied
activity than not wanting downtime. Was her
busyness an attempt to forget the mistakes of
her past? Or was she hoping to do enough good
to cancel them out?

Whatever response she would've given was
cut off when the waitress approached with their
drinks, ready to take their orders.

After she left, Amber smiled. "What about
you? Any eighty-seven-year-old girlfriends?"

He laughed. "No girlfriends of any age."

"So you've never been married? I figured
you'd have a couple of kids by now."

"No kids."

At his terse tone, her gaze snapped upward
and locked with his. It had been four years
and every time he thought about it, the knife
still twisted in his gut. Yeah, he'd been married, until a simple trip to the grocery store had
left his wife dead and some thug ten dollars

richer. Not a conversation he wanted to have in a crowded restaurant.

He took a sip of coffee. "Anything since the note on Tuesday?"

"No. I checked with the others and no one else got anything." She pulled her lower lip between her teeth. "My brother's pretty worried. I'm a little freaked out, too. Hunter's afraid that since I'm the only one who got the note, it means I'm next. But it may not mean anything. The killer didn't give Ramona or Alex any warning."

"Maybe he did and they didn't take it seriously enough to report it."

She picked up her still steeping tea and wrapped both hands around the mug, as if trying to absorb its warmth. His chest clenched. It would take more than hot tea to dispel the chill that had likely been with her since the reunion.

"Do you have someone you can stay with? Hunter, maybe?"

She lifted a brow. "Me and my five cats? Don't worry. I won't open my door without my weapon in my hand, and I fully intend to avoid balconies."

He frowned. "You're assuming he's going to attack in the same way. There are dozens of ways to kill someone. You can't anticipate them all."

"I'm not letting my guard down."

Yeah, and it was affecting her sleep if the shadows beneath her eyes were any indication. "I know I asked you this earlier, but can you think of anyone who might want to see you guys dead, other than Logan?"

She shook her head. "I still think it's Logan. I mean, he was gone for almost ten years. He returns and all this stuff starts. His comment at Walmart was pretty incriminating, too—'Two down, four to go.'"

Good points. But she was discounting Logan's alibi. "When Alex fell, Logan was there, but the night Ramona was killed, he wasn't anywhere near Fort Lauderdale."

"According to Danielle."

"True." No one could corroborate her testimony. Their tryst had been so discreet, none of the neighbors had seen them all weekend. Danielle had claimed she'd brought Logan home late Friday night and parked her car in the garage. They'd slipped out Sunday morning, just before dawn, well before her husband had arrived home from his business trip. Either they'd been really diligent about keeping their affair a secret or they were both lying.

He took a sip of his coffee. "You think she's covering for him?"

"I don't know."

"If she is, she's risking her marriage to do it. If the cat isn't out of the bag now, it will be soon."

Amber crossed her arms. "Assuming the killer is Logan, he obviously has help. A woman wearing gloves and sequined ballet slippers delivered my note."

Caleb nodded. "Then she disappeared. Or got rid of the slippers and gloves."

They'd asked everyone at the reunion, including the staff and caterers, and no one had seen a woman fitting that description. There'd been no witnesses in the bathroom, either. According to Amber, someone had come out as she was going in, and other than the stall at the end being occupied, the bathroom had been empty.

Caleb drummed his fingers on the table. "We're keeping an eye on Logan anyway. Maybe we'll expand that to Danielle."

The waitress returned to set steaming plates of eggs in front of them. Amber picked up a piece of toast and dipped it into her yolk. "If Logan has a female accomplice, it would explain Mona opening the door."

"Who could he have recruited?

"Maybe an old girlfriend of Landon's." She paused. "Danielle dated him before she dated Logan. When Landon dumped her, she took it hard. We wondered whether she was going out with Logan to make Landon jealous."

Caleb put a forkful of scrambled eggs in his mouth and followed it with a sip of coffee. "Do you still have your high school yearbooks?"

"They're stored on the shelf with my old photo albums."

"Good." His were somewhere in his parents' attic. He'd left for college right after high school and gotten married as soon as he'd finished the academy. Picking up childhood memorabilia had never been high on his priority list.

"I'd like to go through them with you, see if they spur any memories. I'm also going to compile a list of everyone who attended the reunion. I want you guys to look at it and point out anyone who dated Landon. Or anyone who may have had a serious crush on him, even if those feelings weren't returned."

She gave him a wry smile. "That was half the school. The female half, anyway. Landon was pretty popular."

"That's a lot of suspects."

Caleb's cell phone buzzed at his hip. One glance at the screen sent adrenaline pumping through him. Frank Mason. The lead detective on the case wouldn't be calling him if it wasn't important.

Frank moved right to business. "I'm aware

you're off, but I thought you'd want to know. We got a call from Vincent Mahoney's wife. Olivia Chamberlain contacted him early this morning and asked him to meet her at McDonald's in Williston. He never arrived."

As Frank talked, Caleb's gut tightened. When his gaze met Amber's, she was watching him, brow creased. She could probably hear every word. *Undertone* wasn't in the man's vocabulary.

Caleb returned his attention to the detective. "Was anyone watching him?" The authorities didn't have around-the-clock surveillance on the four of them, but it was pretty close, especially at night.

"According to Jessica Mahoney, Vincent told the deputy to make sure he wasn't being followed then go back and watch his wife. He hasn't let her out of his sight since this started."

Caleb tightened his grip on the phone. The man was ensuring his wife's safety and may have lost his own life in the process. "I'll let Amber know. I'm sure she'll want to be there. I'll probably tag along."

He ended the call and looked at Amber. Her face had lost three shades of color. He squelched an urge to jump up and wrap her in a comforting hug. Instead he reached across the table to lay his hand over hers. "You probably gathered that wasn't good news."

She swallowed hard, the muscles in her neck moving with the action. "Vincent's gone."

"We don't know for sure. Would you like a ride to the Mahoneys'?"

She nodded. "I'm sure Liv will head over there. If possible, I'd like to be with both of them when they get the news." Her gaze shifted to stare at some point beyond him. "Liv is going to blame herself, since she was the one he was going to meet."

Sadness settled in her eyes, mixed with a good dose of regret. Although she spoke of Liv, her thoughts were obviously in the past. His impression at the Gathering Table had been correct. Amber had been beating herself up for the past ten years. She still wasn't through.

He squeezed her hand. "Sometimes bad things happen because of our actions, even though they were completely innocent at the time." How well he knew.

She pulled her hand from beneath his. "I need to get over to Jessica's."

He signaled the waitress for their check. He'd eaten all but his toast, and Amber had made it through most of her breakfast. But they were finished. Frank's phone call had seen to that.

After paying for their meals, he led Amber toward his truck.

With God's help, he'd finally found a measure of peace. He'd gradually let go of the blame and accepted healing.

Maybe he could help Amber do the same.

FIVE

"I wonder how Vince's wife is holding up." Amber stared through the front windshield, her expression thoughtful. She'd been quiet during most of the trip, but Caleb hadn't tried to engage her in conversation. She was looking at the likelihood of having lost another friend.

She crossed her arms in front of her. "You know, he's the only one of us who's married. As far as I know, Alex never got married. Ramona did, but that ended." She looked over at him. "Raymond's too much of a party guy to ever get married. And Liv is just… Liv."

"What about you?"

"Someday maybe. Right now I've got too much going on. I don't have time to put into a relationship. That's how it's been for a while. In college, I was too busy trying to keep up with my studies while working almost full-time. My grades weren't good enough to get scholarships." She uncrossed her arms and let her hands rest in her lap. "I had plenty of time to date when I was in high school, but my dad was a pretty big deterrent."

Caleb grinned over at her. He'd never asked Amber out, but he could imagine that of Mr. Kingston.

"He had a knack for scaring the guys away, or at least freaking them out pretty good with his demands. Any prospective suitors had to come inside, sit down and have a polite conversation with him and Mom. It didn't take Dad long to get to *the talk*—how to treat a girl with respect and not try to take advantage."

"Just what most sixteen-and seventeen-year-old guys want to hear."

"Yeah. Word got around and it cut down on the traffic. But thinking about a few of those guys, I wasn't missing much."

Caleb turned into the driveway indicated by his GPS. A ritzy house stood at the end, surrounded by several sprawling acres. Olivia's older-model Fiat wasn't there. But the Alachua County sheriff's cruiser looked conspicuously out of place sitting next to the fountain. Reminders of the ugliness of society didn't belong in picture-perfect settings.

Caleb stepped from the truck then walked with Amber on the brick pavers leading to the front door. The house was stucco, with multiple gables and alcoves and other architectural accents. The porch spanned the entire two stories, a crystal chandelier hanging twelve feet below its peak. They were several miles southwest of Gainesville and were about to see firsthand some of those pleasures referred to in Vincent's line of the poem.

A half minute after he rang the bell, one of the huge double doors swung inward and a woman who resembled Jessica stood in the opening.

Amber stepped forward. "I'm Amber Kingston, a friend of Vince, and this is Caleb Lyons with Levy County Sheriff."

The woman stepped back to allow them entrance. "I'm Julia, Jessica's sister."

She led them through a marble-tiled foyer and down two steps into a sunken living room. A huge Oriental rug occupied the center, with leather couches and chairs arranged around the edges. A uniformed deputy stood near one corner. Julia eased down next to Jessica, who sat on one of the couches, her head in her hands.

Amber claimed the empty spot on her other side and wrapped an arm around her shoulders. "We came as soon as we heard. Any news?"

Jessica lifted her tear-streaked face. "They found his car along 121, but there's been no sign of him." Fresh tears gathered on her lower lashes. "I didn't want him to go."

The deputy left the room and moments later the front door opened and closed. He'd probably decided his bodyguard services weren't needed. At least not inside the house.

Caleb took one of the adjacent chairs. "Did he say what Liv wanted?"

"He said she was upset and needed to talk. I asked him to not go. I didn't see why she couldn't say what she needed to say over the phone. He said Liv needed him. That long ago they'd made a vow to stick together and he wouldn't renege on it now."

Caleb nodded. He knew all about the vow. For ten years, all six of them had kept the secret, until he'd convinced Amber to come clean. Had Vincent shared that with his wife? Probably not.

"What time did Liv call?"

Julia reached for her sister's hands. "They've already asked her all the questions. I don't think she needs any more interrogation."

Jessica held up a hand. In the other, she clutched a tissue. "I'd rather talk. If I sit here and do nothing, I'll go stark raving mad."

She dabbed at her eyes then dropped both hands into her lap. "It was around six thirty. I would have gone with him, but I'd just gotten up. He's an early riser and always goes for a morning jog. He told me not to rush, that he'd run out and be back in an hour. Liv had asked him to meet her at the McDonald's in Williston, which is an easy drive down 121."

"When did you first fear something was wrong?"

"Vince promised he'd call when he was leaving McDonald's. That way I'd know he was going to be home in twenty minutes."

She drew in a shaky breath. "When it got to be seven forty-five, I called him and it went to voice mail." She looked at Amber. "I didn't have any of your numbers. They were all in Vince's phone. So I called the police."

The doorbell chimed and Julia rose and left the room. Moments later she returned with Olivia, who hurried across the room to sit next to Jessica and wrap her in a tearful hug. Jessica stiffened, but Olivia seemed not to notice.

"I'm so sorry. I should never have called Vince. I had no idea something could happen between here and Williston." She released Jessica and wiped her eyes. "I needed to talk to someone. Everything that's been going on has me scared to death. I feel like we're being hunted." She shuddered. "Last night I had an awful nightmare. It wouldn't go away. So I called Vince."

Julia took a seat in a nearby chair and Olivia released a moan. "I thought he was taking too long. So when I couldn't get hold of him, I called the police." She stopped her flow of words to wipe her eyes again. "While they were talking to me at McDonald's, a message came in over the radio that they'd found Vince's car on the side of the road. If he's been killed, I'll never forgive myself."

Jessica remained silent, her posture still stiff. She was obviously not pleased with the other woman's presence. For good reason. She'd tried to stop Vince from leaving, but he'd put his friendship with Olivia over the wishes of his wife.

Caleb shifted his gaze to where a fireplace graced the opposite wall. Glass shelves framed it on both sides. The vases and figurines there were probably valued at more than his annual salary. Likely, none of the opulence meant anything to Jessica at the moment.

Olivia continued. "Maybe his car broke down and he set out walking." False optimism filled her words.

Caleb frowned. She was grasping at straws. If Vincent broke down, he would've used his cell phone. If he'd had no service and had set out walking, someone would have found him.

But if he was dead…there were a lot of

woods along State Road 121 between the Mahoney home and Williston. Authorities were likely already combing them.

He pushed himself up from the couch and headed toward the front door. When he stepped outside, the deputy was sitting in his car. The sun was halfway to its apex, promising yet another scorching day.

Caleb released a heavy breath. Those fishing plans he'd had this morning seemed light-years away. It wasn't even ten o'clock and it had already been a long day.

The deputy waved then reached for his radio. A few seconds later he stepped from the vehicle. Judging from the set of his jaw, he didn't have good news.

He closed the car door. "They found the victim in the woods about a quarter mile from his car."

"And?"

"Shot in the back of the head, execution style."

Caleb cringed then watched the deputy shuffle toward the porch. Notifying victims was always the worst part of the job.

He turned to follow. He'd leave the unpleasant task to the deputy. But Amber was inside that house. Vincent's death would hit her hard.

It also meant the killer was one step closer to

his goal. Three of the original six friends were gone. Only three were left.

He needed to confront Olivia and Raymond with the information Amber had given him last night. He was convinced Amber had told him everything she knew. He was equally convinced the others were keeping secrets, both from him and from their one-time friend.

What were they hiding?

Had they followed through with their plans to beat Landon up and gotten carried away? Had they put someone else up to it?

What actually happened that night ten years ago?

Amber sped down Hodges Avenue, happy to have something to occupy her thoughts. The events of Thursday morning had haunted her for the past two days. Vincent gone. Shot in the head. Jessica left with a big, beautiful home and no one to share it with.

And Liv, having to forever deal with the knowledge that her phone call to Vince had led to his death.

Olivia had never been the most emotionally secure of them. With an alcoholic father who'd taken off when she was a baby and a string of stepfathers who hadn't given her the time of day, she was always grasping for attention. When things didn't go her way, her reactions seemed over the top, as if she was one step away from a nervous breakdown. Amber wasn't sure what was for show and what was real.

Recent events were clearly taking their toll. Her hysteria at the reunion was just the beginning. Amber had already fielded several panicked phone calls, two of which had come in in the past two days. The situation with Vincent was about to push Liv over the edge.

She tapped the brakes and turned onto 166th Court. She was only a block from her house. But home would have to wait. A call had come in a few minutes ago, someone shooting off fireworks behind the Cedar Key Museum. Hunter was right behind her, following in the department's SUV. Her chief and her annoying big brother were taking the threats against her seriously.

Actually she was taking them pretty seriously herself.

This one was probably nothing more than a little Saturday night rowdiness, teenagers getting a jump on their Independence Day celebrations. But what they were detonating was likely illegal.

She braked to a stop in the museum's parking lot. As soon as she opened the door, a boom broke the stillness and a vertical streak lit the space beyond the museum building. Yep, definitely illegal.

She stepped from the car and clicked on her flashlight. Darkness had fallen some time ago. She was into the tenth hour of her usual eight-hour shift. But one officer was on vacation and another had contracted a summertime bug. So the rest of them were putting in extra time.

As she moved with Hunter down the wide sidewalk bordering the museum building, she swept the beam of her flashlight over the area. Ahead, a huge metal bowl stood just past where the concrete ended, a Confederate salt kettle on display. To the left, a curved brick walk led to the Whitman House, nestled against the woods. The soft glow of its porch lights didn't reach where they stood.

Hunter held up a hand and clicked off his flashlight. She did the same, casting them in near blackness. The scent of smoke lingered in the air but the night was quiet except for the whisper of a breeze through the trees. The suspects had probably lit one last rocket then taken off.

Hunter clicked his flashlight on and continued down the sidewalk. A twig snapped nearby. She whirled toward the woods, eyes straining for any sign of movement. Hunter stopped, too, then moved in that direction. Perspiration dotted her forehead and she reached up to swipe it away. The afternoon shower that had blown through around five o'clock had turned the entire island into a sauna rather than providing a respite from the heat.

But the sticky Florida humidity wasn't the only reason she was sweating. Unease draped around her, a sense of being watched. Weapon in her right hand and flashlight in the other, she stepped off the sidewalk to follow Hunter past the house. In the woods, the darkness was thick. There was no moon, and clouds obscured the stars.

For the next fifteen minutes the two of them combed the area. Finally, Hunter headed back toward the museum building.

"Apparently whoever was here earlier has left."

She looked up at him in the darkness. If he believed that, he wouldn't be whispering. When they stepped from the trees, she pointed toward the rear of the building some distance away. "That's where the bottle rocket or Roman candle went up when we first arrived."

As they made their way past the salt kettle, Hunter's flashlight beam stopped its sweeping movement to lock in on some small objects. Some kind of debris was lying on the ground behind the building. She stepped forward to study the items illuminated by the flashlight. A couple of burned-up cylinders lay at her feet, along with remnants of paper, several long sticks and cardboard with singed edges.

The scene was comforting in an odd sort of way. Through her teen years, she and her friends had shot off more than their fair share of fireworks. It was amazing they still had all their fingers.

She smiled up at Hunter. This call was what it appeared to be. "Looks like we interrupted someone's pre–Independence Day celebration."

"I'd say you're right." He nudged one of the items with his foot.

A faint sizzle sounded somewhere behind her. As she spun, an explosion rent the air and a ball of fire lit up the darkness. Heat seared her left shoulder and she grasped it with her other hand, stumbling sideways.

Hunter tackled her, bringing her to the ground behind the kettle. After swiping his fingers down her ponytail, he gave her arm a few rough pats. "Are you hurt?"

"I'm fine. Go after him."

He hesitated. "Are you sure?"

She pushed him away from her. "I'll call for backup. Go."

Hunter sprang to his feet and jogged toward

the woods. Still crouched behind the kettle, she snatched her radio from her belt. When she'd finished her call, she walked into the woods where Hunter had disappeared a minute earlier.

The killer was likely nearby. What just happened wasn't a case of carelessness. Someone had intentionally fired a bottle rocket at her. If she'd taken a direct hit, instead of the flare grazing her shoulder, she'd have been seriously injured.

Even now, her right palm felt as if she held a handful of stinging nettles instead of her pistol grip, and her shoulder throbbed with heat. Judging from the way Hunter had patted her upper arm, her shirt sleeve had likely been smoldering.

He'd swiped a hand down her ponytail, too. She reached up to feel the tresses—silky until she got to their ends. Dry and brittle, they disintegrated in her hand. Apparently when she'd spun, her hair had swung around and gotten hit at the same time as her shoulder. She was hurt, but tonight could have turned out so much worse. A little higher and to the right, and she'd have been hit in the face.

In the distance, beams of light flashed through the trees, Hunter searching for the suspect. Soon sirens sounded, drawing closer. More law enforcement would come from the mainland, Levy County lending aid. Authorities were likely already setting up a road block on 24. It was the only way on and off Cedar Key. Unless one had a boat.

An hour later she pulled into the station's parking lot. They hadn't found anyone near the museum and no one suspicious had tried to leave Cedar Key. She parked the cruiser and got out to circle her SUV. It had been sitting there for the past eleven hours, but no one had placed any notes on the windshield. She blew out a relieved breath. As she continued down the passenger side, she gasped.

On the rear side window was a familiar message, sinister in its simplicity. "One by one" spelled out with what looked like white shoe polish.

Hunter hurried over to stand next to her. "'One by one.' It seems to be the killer's motto." He draped an arm across her shoulders and pulled her against his side in a protective bigbrother hug. "Why is he singling you out for these warnings? Why not just strike?"

"I don't know." Sometimes killers got a thrill out of taunting law enforcement. That was common in scenarios like this. But this wasn't a game, an opportunity to pit his wit and skill against that of the police. This was revenge, pure and simple.

The killer believed they'd all murdered Landon. But she was the one who'd set the whole thing in motion. She was the guiltiest of all. So death alone wasn't enough. He had to torment her first.

Hunter gave her another squeeze then guided her toward the door of the station. "Let's get our reports written. Then I'll follow you home."

She nodded. No use trying to argue with him. Besides, she didn't relish the thought of going into the house alone. Since the threats had been left at the station, the killer apparently didn't know where she lived. But in a community the size of Cedar Key, it would only be a matter of time.

When she arrived home a short time later, Hunter pulled in right behind her and stepped from his truck. She looked around and gave him a cautious smile. "No boogeymen."

"None out here. I'm going to check inside."

"I think I'm capable of that. I *am* a cop, you know."

"First and foremost, you're my sister. I'm checking inside."

"Bossy much?" Actually he'd always been. It didn't annoy her as much now as it had when they were kids. Sometimes she wished she'd have listened.

She turned the key in the lock and opened

the front door, careful not to let any cats escape. Two occupied the couch and two shared the love seat. Tippy was stretched out on one of the upper shelves of the entertainment center, lying against a row of DVDs.

As she closed and locked the door, all five eyed Hunter warily, but not with enough concern to give up their comfy seats. Since she'd taken care of them during her dinner break, they were all full and happy.

Hunter walked into the kitchen then doubled back toward the two bedrooms. Instead of following, she greeted each cat. Down the hall, a closet door slid open on its track and closed again.

When he returned a few minutes later she straightened to face him. "Feel better now?"

"Not really." He frowned. "Come and stay with Meagan and me."

She made a wide sweep of her arm, indicating the five fur balls staring at her from different places around the room. Cimba took the motion as an invitation and jumped down to approach.

"Take them back to the shelter."

"There isn't room." She bent to pick up the yellow tabby weaving in and out of her legs. The cat nuzzled her chin and began to purr. Soon both front paws were kneading air.

Smokey, Ash and Shadow left their lounging places to plead for the attention Cimba had garnered. Tippy paused then returned to grooming herself. She craved love, too, but without the desperation the others displayed.

Amber placed Cimba on the floor and squatted to pet the other three. She'd promised to keep them until they found permanent homes. She wasn't going to abandon them if she had any choice in the matter.

When she straightened and looked at Hunter, he was still frowning.

"You need to think about yourself for a change."

For a change? Thinking of herself was what she'd done for the first eighteen years of her life. And look at the damage she'd caused. Landon was dead and her dad would never work again.

Although Logan blamed her, her parents never had. Heart problems ran in her dad's family, they'd said. But she blamed herself. She'd heard the doctor's orders. Absolutely no stress. That had been what she'd given him all through high school. Harold had started the process and she'd finished it.

She put a hand on Hunter's shoulder. "He doesn't know where I live. I'm being careful.

I'm armed. And I'm trained. Remember, I went through the same police academy you did."

"You're being targeted."

"If I feel at all threatened here, you'll have a house guest." She led him toward the door. "I'll figure out other arrangements for the cats." Hopefully it wouldn't come to that.

She gave Hunter a hug. "I love you, even though you're overprotective and annoying sometimes."

"I love you, too, even though you're too stubborn for your own good."

When he stepped off the front porch, he turned and motioned toward the door. "Lock that right away."

"Trust me, I will." The killer may not know where she lived, but she wasn't stupid. She'd checked and double checked the windows and doors repeatedly since the reunion.

When Hunter reached his truck, she closed and locked the door, then crossed the room to where Tippy lay. If she had to move in with Hunter in the future, maybe she could take Tippy and keep her closed up in the bedroom. One cat would be doable. Five wouldn't.

She dropped her hand and moved to the couch. Ash and Shadow jumped up to pace back and forth across her lap. Cimba and

Smokey joined them. As she spread her attention between the four, her heart twisted.

Soon she'd call Sheltering Hands and give them a heads-up. She'd have to relinquish the cats eventually. By holding out, she was just delaying the inevitable. The killer wasn't going to give up.

One by one.

The words were no longer on her window. After taking a photo to add to the file, Hunter had cleaned them off with a sponge and soapy water. But they were still engraved clearly in her mind.

One by one. Mona, Alex and now Vince.

She'd promised Hunter that if she felt threatened, she'd make arrangements for the cats and leave.

Something told her that moment might come sooner than she anticipated.

SIX

Caleb eased to a stop in Amber's driveway then laid his sunglasses on the dash. In the rearview mirror, the sun was barely visible over the tops of the trees. He'd driven all the way down Hodges with it shining in his eyes.

After picking up the file folder lying in the passenger seat, he stepped from the truck. A short distance away, an unmarked car sat just off the road. Its presence brought a measure of comfort. There would be a similar sight in Olivia's and Raymond's neighborhoods.

The morning Vincent was killed, the deputy patrolling Olivia's neighborhood had been pulled away on another call. Fortunately for her, the killer had focused his attention on Vincent. Now all three of them had twenty-four-hour protection. And no one was to go anywhere without a law enforcement escort.

Caleb closed the door of the truck and walked toward the house. As before, the blinds were drawn, but no cats occupied the windowsills. There was no need to keep watch. The cat lady was in residence.

He smiled at the image that popped into his mind—a little old lady with a fur ball occupying every flat surface. Except Amber only had five. And she was hardly a little old lady.

After he rang the bell, the blinds at the nearest window separated. A moment later the door swung inward. Amber motioned him inside, using her foot to block the path of a black cat that looked ready to bolt. Three others lay on the couch, their eyes alert. The fifth was on the dining room table, the one she called Tippy.

Amber locked the door behind him. "I figured you'd want to come at a different time. With church this morning, you couldn't have gotten much sleep."

"I managed a few hours and even grabbed some supper."

"Good." She gave him a half smile but her features held tension.

"Are you okay?"

"Chief Sandlin called me. I have another poem."

"When? Where?"

"Taped to the door of the police station, in an envelope with my name on it. This one's short, only two lines. Our killer's getting lazy." She laughed, but it sounded hollow.

"What does it say?"

"'Three down, three to go. Who's next? You don't know.'"

A block of ice replaced the hot dinner he'd finished a half hour earlier. *Three down, three to go.* Logan's words to Amber in the Walmart parking lot. Only the numbers had changed. She'd probably made the connection, too.

"We've got guys tailing Logan. We're keeping a pretty close eye on Danielle, too. But I don't think you should be staying alone."

"That's what Hunter says. He's pressuring me to move in with him and Meagan."

"I think you should listen."

"It's complicated."

"Have Liv or Raymond gotten any threats?"

"Liv hasn't for sure. I talked to her thirty minutes ago. If she'd gotten a note, she'd have been even more freaked out than usual." She crossed her arms and lowered her voice. "I think the killer is singling me out because I'm the one who sent the texts. If it weren't for that, Landon would have stayed home and we wouldn't even be having this discussion."

The words were heavy with regret, sending a pang of sadness straight to his heart. He squeezed her shoulder. "Amber, Landon's death wasn't your fault."

"Someone would beg to differ."

She was right. Someone wasn't letting her off the hook. Unfortunately she wasn't, either. "No rational person would blame you for what happened. You shouldn't try to carry a burden that's not yours."

"Yeah." The word held no conviction. She lifted her shoulders and let them fall, as if shrugging off the malaise hanging over her. "Let's get this done."

She led him toward the couch. All three cats jumped down before he even rounded the end of the coffee table, joining the black one to watch him from across the room. Tippy didn't relinquish her spot.

After sitting, he pulled some sheets from the file folder. "I have a list of everyone who attended the reunion."

"And I have yearbooks." She sank onto the couch next to him and took one from the small stack on the coffee table. "My senior year."

She laid the book in her lap. Her shoulder and arm rested against his. So did her uniform-clad leg. Warmth radiated from her. It had been a long time since he'd sat this close to a beautiful woman. Four years, to be precise. And the experience left him with an odd mix of contentment and longing.

He tamped down both. This was strictly business. She'd sat close so he could see the pictures with her. And the fact that his thoughts were heading in other directions proved how much the loneliness was getting to him.

Amber opened the cover of the yearbook. Inscriptions filled the space. The outline of a red heart occupied most of the adjacent page and he scanned the words scrawled inside. "High school's been a blast. Adulthood's going to be even funner. Don't let the party end!" It was signed "Liv."

Amber turned to the next page. She'd agreed to look through the yearbooks with him. That didn't mean she wanted him reading personal messages from her friends.

She flipped to the beginning of the senior class and pointed to a picture of a smiling brunette. "Becky Adams. She dated Landon for a while."

Yeah, he remembered her. She was one of the cheerleaders. He'd also had a geometry class with her.

Amber tapped the picture. "I don't know who dumped who, but I don't think it lasted long. You probably knew her better than I did, since you went to the games, being in band and all."

He nodded. "If I remember right, she didn't seem too broken up over it." He opened the file folder. Becky Adams's name was on the list, except she was now Becky Adams Sharpe. He removed a pen from his pocket and put a plus next to her name.

"What's that for?"

"Dated Landon but not high on the suspect list. I'll star the ones to talk to first."

She nodded and pointed to another picture. "Lucy Beckman. According to Liv, she and Landon were an item for a while."

"I didn't know her well."

"We called her Loosie Lucy. She got around."

That was what he'd heard. The girls joked about her reputation and the guys took advantage of it. "Probably not someone who'd have been brokenhearted over their split."

When he turned the page, Olivia Chamberlain stared up at them from the right-hand side. In that picture, she was a platinum-blonde and wearing enough makeup to beautify the entire cheerleading squad.

The Cleary brothers' photos were in the row below. Though the resemblance was strong, they weren't identical twins. Landon's hair was much darker than his brother's and the somewhat square Cleary jaw on Landon was smoothed out on Logan.

Those weren't the only differences. Logan's eyes projected a seriousness and quiet intelligence. He'd always been contemplative, the type to think things through. And apparently not one to forget a wrong.

Landon had been the opposite. Even in a ten-year-old photo, that air of carefree popularity was obvious, the look of someone who had the world by the tail. Someone who had everything to live for.

As they worked their way through the photos, they identified several more girls who'd carried a torch for Landon. Amber had colorful stories about most of them, and he continued to add pluses and stars to his list.

"Danielle Harcourt." She pointed at the page. "She should get a double star."

"You said she was pretty upset when Landon dumped her."

"Shortly after they broke up, Liv said she found Danielle in the bathroom crying."

She turned the page and he tilted his head.

"That's a good picture of you." In that shot, her makeup was understated and her hair fell in silken waves about her shoulders. She apparently hadn't done anything beyond her normal beauty routine. As long as he'd known her, she'd never gone to extremes to stand out, a trait he found appealing.

But as pretty as she was, the rebellious streak that wove through her came out in the picture—the lift of her chin, the one-sided smile. He could even see it in her eyes, a silent show of defiance. Now it was all gone, replaced with determination underscored by sadness.

Several pages later, her index finger settled beneath one of the photos. "Kindall Osborne. You guys dated all the way through high school. Everyone thought for sure you were going to end up married."

"We did."

At his whispered words, she pivoted her head to look at him.

The first time she'd broached the subject they'd been in a crowded restaurant. Now they were alone and he still had no desire to tell the story. His relationship with Amber was strictly professional. She didn't need the details of his love life.

"I'm sorry it didn't work out." She dropped her gaze to the yearbook.

By the time they'd pointed out everyone who'd dated Landon, they'd hit almost every letter of the alphabet, some more than once. Not all of the girls had come to the reunion, but many had. The ones that hadn't, he added to the bottom of the list. He wouldn't rule them out yet.

Amber indicated his folder. "You've got a good list, but we should probably go through this exercise with Liv. She was the Chiefland High gossip queen. She knew everything about everybody. And didn't mind sharing it."

Yes, he'd do that. He'd already questioned both Liv and Raymond about the rape and the guys' threats. Judging by the long pause on the other end of the line, his question had caught Raymond off guard. When he recovered, his answer had echoed Amber's. They'd been drunk and just talking tough. He'd even had an explanation for his parents saying he was in before one in the morning when the police report showed him out with his brother almost an hour later. He'd claimed the two of them had sneaked back out.

Liv's response had been more emotional. Whether she'd been upset over the rape itself or the fact that Amber had spilled her secret, he wasn't sure. She'd insisted she didn't want to talk about it. She finally reiterated what Amber had said, that she didn't think the others had been planning to follow through with their threats. But after both conversations, he still hadn't been able to shake the feeling they were hiding something.

The two gray cats hopped up next to Amber. Over the past several minutes they'd crept gradually closer, keeping cautious eyes on him. Apparently their need for affection had overcome their fear of a strange man in their domain.

When Amber lifted her hand to pet them, the final pages fell to the left, leaving the inside cover exposed. Landon had scrawled a message in the top right corner then signed his name in fancy script, the bottom of the *L* curling around to wrap the rest of the letters. To the right of his name was a small treble clef.

Caleb grinned. "'To the sexiest lab partner I ever had'?"

She returned his smile. "We had biology together my senior year. You remember how we had to switch lab partners every six weeks? The last six-week period, I was with Landon. I did all the drawings and reports and let him do the dissecting."

"Sounds like a fair trade."

"Worked out great for me, anyway. Just the smell of the formaldehyde about finished me off. I was happy to let someone else do the cutting."

"Did you have any other classes with him?"

"Not my senior year. Liv did, though. Algebra. She talked about it a lot. She struggled with it and since Landon got straight As, she'd regularly ask him for help. A bunch of times he stayed late to work with her on an assignment."

She closed the book and set it on the table. "That year we really got to know Landon. At least, we thought we did." She shook her head. "Finding out he raped Liv floored me. He seemed like such a nice guy."

The news had shocked him, too. Besides having taken several classes with Landon, they'd been in band together all through high school. Caleb had always liked the guy.

So had everyone else. He was the all-American teenager, full of school spirit—class president, homecoming king, first chair trumpet and member of several clubs. His murder had shaken not only his classmates but the entire community. Someone had made a sign in his memory and placed it along 341, near where his body had been found. For months mounds of flowers had adorned its base. Other signs kept popping up at random places, with messages like We Remember Landon Cleary and Bring Landon's Killer to Justice.

Caleb closed the folder and laid it on top of the yearbook. "How well did you know Logan?"

"Not as well as Landon. Logan took a lot of the advanced placement classes." She gave him a wry smile. "You probably remember, I avoided those. I think Logan and I only shared one class, an English class our sophomore year. I don't remember communicating with him much or getting to know him. He seemed pretty serious, intent on learning." She paused, thinking. "I remember during the poetry section, he..." Her eyes grew wide.

"What?"

"Logan writes poetry."

His pulse picked up. "He does?"

"He did then. For about a month of that class we studied poetry. We had to write several ourselves and Logan wrote some really good ones. When the teacher would ask people to read what they'd written, he'd always volunteer."

"All the killer's notes have been in poetry form." That in itself wasn't a very strong connection, but when considered with everything else, it justified further investigation.

Over the years, Logan had made it clear that he blamed each of them for his brother's death. The killings had begun within weeks of his arriving home after being discharged from the military. The last poem echoed his words to Amber in the Walmart parking lot. No one could corroborate his alibi for the weekend Ramona was killed except Danielle, who could be lying to protect him. Or maybe he was in cahoots with someone else. If so, he may have left a trail in his phone or email records.

Did they have enough for a judge to grant

them a search warrant? Maybe, maybe not. He'd pass along this latest bit of info and it would go up the chain of command.

"Thanks for going through these with me."

"No problem. Sometimes it's fun to reminisce. I haven't thought about some of these people in years."

A ringtone sounded from the kitchen and she excused herself. Four cats followed her. If they were anything like his monsters, they probably thought anytime someone walked into the kitchen, it was time to eat.

He picked up the second yearbook. There was no reason to go through the others, even though Amber had gotten them out. Anyone not included their senior year likely didn't have any valuable information.

As he let the book fall open to the center, Amber's soft hello drifted to him. He turned the page and looked at the group picture of the band. He was in the center row to the left. Landon was two rows behind, to the right.

The volume of Amber's voice rose. "Liv, calm down. I can't understand you."

He set the book aside as Amber continued. "Have you called the police?"

Caleb stood. When he reached the kitchen, Amber was pacing. "Good. Until he gets back, keep your doors locked and stay away from the windows. Where are you now?" She paused. "The bathroom is good. Wait there for the deputy. Is there someone you can stay with tonight?"

Liv spoke again and Amber nodded. "All right. Call me as soon as he's done."

Amber lowered the phone. "Someone tried to get into Liv's house. When she wouldn't answer the knock on the back door, he fired shots through one of the rear windows. All this with a deputy sitting in the vacant lot across the street."

"Where's the deputy now?"

"He came running when he heard the shots. After making sure Liv was okay, he went in pursuit. When he returned, she ended the call."

Amber started to pace again. "I feel I should go over there. Liv is totally freaked out."

He stepped in front of her and placed both hands on her shoulders. "You need to stay here. The same person who's after her is after you. Let Levy County handle it."

Amber nodded. "She's staying with a neighbor tonight."

"Good." He hoped she wasn't putting an innocent bystander at risk. But she shouldn't stay alone until the killer was caught. Amber shouldn't, either. He'd suggest they stay together, except Liv would probably drive Amber crazy.

When the same ringtone sounded, Amber swiped the screen and put the phone to her ear. Judging from her side of the conversation, the deputy hadn't found anyone. The killer seemed to have a knack for disappearing into thin air.

Caleb watched Amber as she spoke. Her brows drew together.

"That's probably not a good idea. Maybe you can come over here and hang out. I'm off. We can stay inside." She paused before continuing. "I understand. But until this guy is caught, we can't be traipsing around like tourists." Her eyes widened. "Unless…let me talk to Caleb and I'll call you back."

Caleb's stomach drew into a knot. "I don't know what you have in mind, but I'm pretty sure I'm not going to like it."

"Liv wants to get away, hang out at the beach, maybe even rent one of those two-man kayaks."

His stomach twisted into a knot. "No way."

"This creep is going to strike again. We just don't know when or where. This way, we'd be calling the shots. If he thinks Liv and I are vulnerable, he might make a move. We'll have a chance of catching him before anyone else gets killed."

What she said made sense, but he still didn't like it. "You'd be bait."

"We're bait anyway." She leaned against the

counter and spread her arms, palms against the laminate surface. "You and Hunter can come along. We've already got law enforcement watching us all the time, anyway. With a little coordination, we could set a trap."

He heaved a sigh of resignation. "This isn't my decision to make. I'll see what everyone thinks."

After bidding her farewell, he walked to his truck, his gait stiff. What Amber had in mind was risky. But so was waiting and doing nothing. He and Hunter would be armed and alert. Amber would be, too. They'd have undercover people around the beach and on the water. Everything would be open, so there'd be no opportunity for the killer to hide and take potshots from the woods.

As he drove away from Cedar Key, the tightness gradually released its grip on his chest. Maybe this was what it would take to solve the case. Besides, spending the day with Amber had a lot of appeal, even though he'd be sharing the experience with Hunter and Liv. And a half dozen other law enforcement personnel.

Or maybe it was *because* he was sharing the experience with the others. There'd be no expectations, no misunderstandings—no way it could be mistaken for a date.

He stifled a snort. Who was he kidding?

There wouldn't be any misunderstandings on Amber's part. She had her job, her animals and her volunteer activities. She didn't have time for a relationship. She'd already told him that.

No, it was his thoughts that kept drifting in that direction. The self-imposed loneliness was starting to get old.

It had been four years. Maybe it was time. Maybe he should tell God that if He had a woman picked out for him, he might be open to the idea.

It would take some getting used to. He'd move slowly. And God's direction would have to be clear.

Just please don't let her be a cop.

The bell chimed and Amber crossed the room to swing open the door. Liv stood on her porch. The tank and cutoff jean shorts she wore made Amber's shorts and T-shirt seem like granny clothes in comparison. But whatever message Liv's clothing choices relayed, creases of worry lined her face. She'd likely gotten little sleep last night.

Amber closed the door and led Liv into the living room where Hunter and Caleb waited. The cats had already disappeared. Three people occupying their space were two too many.

Amber took a seat next to Caleb and Liv positioned herself near Hunter. Both guys were wearing their tourist label well with their khaki shorts and polo shirts. Caleb's was an aqua blue that deepened the already amazing color of his eyes. His sandy-blond hair was casually tossed but not messy, further adding to his appeal.

Okay, maybe "male model" would be more fitting than "tourist."

Caleb leaned forward to rest his forearms on his legs and entwine his fingers. "Since everyone's here, I have some things to go over with you." His serious, no-nonsense tone didn't fit with their plans for a day of fun and relaxation. "Hunter and I will stay on alert, but we'll also have several other sets of eyes on you ladies. While we're kayaking, a couple of guys will be fishing from a powerboat." He grinned. "We had no problem getting volunteers for that undercover assignment."

He leaned back but didn't unclasp his hands. "We've also got someone on Atsena Otie Key. We'll rent the kayaks right there by the park, paddle out and circle the island."

Liv grinned. "You sure know how to take the spontaneity out of an outing."

Caleb ignored the teasing criticism. "Between our guys on the water and the one strolling the island, we should be able to spot any suspicious activity."

As Caleb talked, Liv popped her gum. She had one leg crossed over the other, her foot swinging in a steady rhythm. Instead of boating shoes or flip-flops, she wore sandals with a modest wedge heel, her toenails painted to resemble mini watermelon slices. "What about this afternoon?"

"After lunch, we'll hike the old Railroad Trestle Trail. One deputy will go ahead of us and the other will watch for anyone going in behind us. Throughout the day, be alert. But relax and have fun. Let law enforcement be your eyes and ears. If the killer thinks your guard is down, he'll be more likely to strike." He looked around the room then stood. "Let's go have some fun. And we'll see if we can catch a killer."

Amber slipped her pistol into the waistband of her shorts and pulled her T-shirt down over it.

Fifteen minutes later they all stood on the beach, two kayaks lying next to them in the sand. Amber picked up her orange life vest and tossed it into a kayak. A short distance away, Atsena Otie broke the surface of the Gulf, a green, tree-covered mass. According to Caleb, someone was already there, posing as a tourist, strolling the beach. Three powerboats bobbed up and down in the gentle swells, one likely holding law enforcement.

Caleb pushed a kayak into the water. After holding it steady so Amber could get in, he joined her.

Soon Liv and Hunter were settled in theirs. Liv had kicked off her shoes and was wearing a wide grin, her eyes sparkling. The stress that had hung over her when she'd arrived seemed to have dissipated. She raised her paddle over her head. "Wanna race?"

"You're on." Caleb's tone held a good dose of competitiveness. "Losers buy the winners lunch."

Amber dug in her paddle, alternating side-to-side in fluid circular motions. She didn't want to lose to her long-time friend, but she especially wouldn't concede to her brother if she could help it. Caleb coordinated his rhythm with hers and their kayak surged forward with each stroke.

Amber glanced at their competition. Liv and Hunter were neck and neck with them, both their faces set in determination. Before long, Amber's shoulders and triceps began to burn. She was in decent shape but her early morning runs didn't prepare her for kayaking, even with the three-pound dumbbells she often carried. In recent days those runs had come to a screeching halt.

Gradually the other kayak moved into the lead. Liv didn't seem to be tiring. The gap broadened and Amber frowned. "Unless they capsize, I think we're buying lunch."

As soon as Hunter and Liv nosed their kayak onto the shore of Atsena Otie, Liv stepped out. "We won." She spun around twice then did a fist pump. The sun slanted through the purple highlights in her hair, creating a glow that matched the joy on her face.

Amber laid her paddle across her lap and let Caleb propel them in. A walk on the beach would be nice. Anything that didn't require the use of her arms.

After pulling both kayaks onto the sand, they set out walking, Amber and Caleb in the lead. She released a contented sigh. A walk on a deserted beach, native flora on her left, the gently rolling Gulf on her right. It had the potential to be quite romantic. Except for her overprotective brother watching from behind. And the fact that their interest in one another was strictly professional.

Soon, Liv moved up to walk next to Amber and Caleb fell back to talk to Hunter. Male voices drifted to her. Police talk. Comfortable conversation for her. Probably not for Liv.

The spring left Liv's step and her shoulders slumped. She'd cast off the cheerfulness the way one removes a mask. "I can't believe Vince is gone now, too. He had everything—money, a great job, a pretty wife and an amazing house." She looked out over the water. "Do you think the killer is out there somewhere watching us?"

Amber scanned the gentle waves. A young couple paddled toward them in red kayaks. A short distance out, two older guys fished from a Carolina Skiff, according to the lettering on the side of the boat. Even farther out, a sail broke the horizon, headed toward blue water.

"It's possible."

"He probably won't try anything while the guys are with us."

Amber cast a glance over her shoulder. The guys were even farther away than she realized. Maybe they were waiting to see if anyone would make a move. Or her meddling big brother was conspiring with Caleb. If she didn't keep a rein on him, he'd soon have Caleb agreeing to be her personal bodyguard.

"Do you ever feel bad about everything?"

Liv's words cut across her thoughts. "What do you mean?"

"Do you regret sending the texts inviting Landon to the woods?"

"Sometimes." She shifted her gaze to the left

where twisted, sun-bleached wood bordered the palmettos and other Florida undergrowth covering the island. In another hour or two, the tide would reach its maximum low and the stretch of beach where they walked would begin to disappear.

Amber released a sigh. "What bothers me the most, though, is that I didn't text him back and tell him not to come."

Liv nodded. "That would bother me, too. If you had texted him, he'd have stayed home and nothing would've happened."

Amber shot her a sideways glance. Was Liv trying to make her feel worse?

She couldn't tell. Her friend was staring straight ahead, her expression distant. Maybe her words were just an observation. Sometimes Liv had no filter.

"When you and I left, I was too drunk to think about texting him back." She crossed her arms. "You know, I haven't touched the stuff since."

Liv gave her a rueful smile. "I'm afraid I can't say the same. It helps me forget. I can pretend, at least for a while, that everything's okay."

Amber's stomach twisted. Several reasons had been behind her own drinking—rebellion, the desire to fit in, the way it made her feel.

Liv's was all of that, but the primary appeal for her was escape from an intolerable home life. She'd left that life behind a long time ago, but she was still trying to escape.

Liv gave a couple of quick shrugs and turned, her face suddenly bright. She'd slipped the mask of happy party girl back into place. "So what's this Railroad Trestle Trail we're going to do this afternoon?"

"It's a raised trail through mangroves and marshland where the old railroad used to be. All that's left of it are some pilings sticking up out of the water at the end of the trail."

"Sounds kind of sad. Then what?"

"That's it. Caleb's got to go home and get in a few hours of sleep before his shift tonight. Hunter will cut out right after lunch. He's scheduled to report at two."

"He won't want to miss lunch, since you and Caleb are paying." Liv's smile was teasing.

Amber couldn't help but smile back. Today's outing was good for Liv. Maybe she'd go back home more able to cope with the fear of being hunted and the constant reminder of long-ago mistakes.

"What about you?" Amber looked over at Liv. "When do you have to report back to work?"

"I'm not working right now. I got laid off last year and haven't found anything…" Her voice trailed off. Maybe her unemployment was a sore subject.

It didn't take Liv long to find another topic. As they moved around the island, Amber listened to her unending flow of words but still stayed alert to their surroundings. So close to low tide, the fishing probably wasn't great, but there were still a few diehards out there casting their lines.

Her gaze snagged on one sitting in a rowboat with a trolling motor on the back. He was shirtless, with stringy, shoulder-length hair pouring out from beneath a wide-brimmed hat. He held a fishing rod in his right hand and a brown bottle in his left, which he raised in silent greeting. Judging from the laid-back demeanor, he wasn't likely their killer.

No one else appeared threatening, either. Everyone seemed to simply be enjoying a summer day on the water.

When they finished kayaking and went to Big Deck for lunch, no one was watching them then, either. The same when they said goodbye to Hunter and headed out on the Railroad Trestle Trail. If the killer was nearby, he wasn't making himself known.

By the time Caleb pulled into her driveway, it was almost four thirty. Liv climbed from the truck and circled the front of the cab.

Amber slid out the driver's side behind Caleb. "We didn't accomplish what we'd hoped, but I had a lot of fun."

"Me, too." Liv approached to wrap her in a hug. "Thanks for everything. I'm dreading going home to my empty house, but this really helped."

The smile Liv wore looked forced and the sadness behind it tugged at Amber's heart. As much as she longed to help her friend, she hadn't found her own answers yet. She watched Liv plod to her Fiat.

Instead of getting into his truck, Caleb walked toward the front porch. "I'm going to make sure everything's okay inside before I leave."

"You and Hunter both. You know, I am capable of clearing a house."

"I know. We'll do it together." He grinned. "I'm your backup."

At least he didn't make her feel incompetent like Hunter sometimes did. She unlocked the door and he followed her inside. After they'd checked the house, he met her back in the living room.

"Speaking of your brother, it looks like I'll be coming to your family's July Fourth celebration."

Just what she'd thought. While Liv had been

talking her ear off, Hunter had been securing babysitting services. Her stomach quivered with an odd mix of annoyance over Hunter's interference and anticipation at the thought of spending the day with Caleb. She curbed the latter.

"My brother tends to stick his nose in where it doesn't belong. Please don't feel obligated."

"I'm off the Fourth. The third, too. It's my weekend. And I can't think of a better way to spend my holiday."

"I'm guessing Hunter wanted you to drive me to Ocala and back and guard me with your life while I'm there."

He grinned. "Something like that."

She'd kill him later. Or maybe thank him. "All right, but I'm driving." It would be her vehicle and her gas.

She cast a glance at the clock in the dining area.

Caleb followed her gaze. "You have plans for tonight?"

"I'm sitting with someone, but I don't have to leave for another hour." She moved to the couch and took a seat.

He sat next to her. "Your eighty-seven-year-old boyfriend?"

"This one's younger. He's only seventy-eight."

"You get around."

Amber turned so she could face him more fully. "Thanks for everything today. I had a great time."

Caleb nodded. "Me, too."

"I could tell Liv did, also. She seemed reluctant to leave."

"I noticed. She'll be fine, though. The deputy is following her home. Once his shift is finished, someone else will take over. She won't be alone."

Amber pulled her lower lip between her teeth. Liv needed more. She needed someone to listen to her when she was upset, someone to comfort her after a nightmare, someone who knew her past and understood her quirks.

"I'm thinking about inviting her to stay with me."

"Is that what you want?"

She lowered her gaze to the floor. No, it wasn't. She'd lived alone for the past six years. Sharing her space with someone else, especially someone as high maintenance as Liv, was going to require a huge adjustment.

She shrugged. "What I want isn't important. It's what Liv needs. Everything's been taking a toll on her. She's never been emotionally strong. She needs someone to help her cope."

"And that someone has to be you."

"Why not? Other than Raymond, I'm the one who's been friends with her the longest."

"Have you talked to Sheltering Hands yet about taking the cats?"

She looked at him sharply. Caleb had a reason for the abrupt subject change.

"Not yet. I haven't gotten around to it."

He continued to study her. She hated it when he looked at her like that, as if he was trying to discern all her secrets.

Disapproval crept into his gaze. "You're working a full-time job, rescuing abandoned cats and comforting the terminally ill and their families. Now you feel compelled to take on Liv's problems. There's a point at which a good thing becomes an obsession."

Annoyance pushed aside the discomfort. "I have a tender spot for animals, especially cats. And I like to help people. There's nothing wrong with that."

"No, there's not. But people do a lot of 'right things' for the wrong reasons. Are you motivated by the simple joy of service? Or are you maintaining a lifestyle of frenzied activity to take your mind off past regrets?"

She pushed herself to her feet and crossed the room. Caleb's words hit too close to the truth. But telling him so would incur more judgment. "You wouldn't understand."

"Don't count on it." The words were barely above a whisper.

She spun to face him. "Don't even try to convince me you know how I feel. The perpetually perfect Caleb Lyons has probably never experienced a moment of regret in his life." Maybe she was being harsh, but she'd had enough of his condemnation.

Caleb rose, too, but instead of approaching her, he began to pace. "It was four years ago, on a Friday evening." His voice was soft, his eyes fixed on the floor. "I'd finished working a double shift. We needed a few groceries. I think my wife was hoping I'd run to the store, but seeing how exhausted I was, she offered to go instead." He stopped walking to look at her, his face lined with sadness.

The air between them was heavy and thick. Whatever annoyance she'd felt earlier had completely dissipated.

Caleb's shoulders slumped and regret settled around him like a cloak. "I should have gone. Or at least have offered to ride along. Instead, I let her go out alone in the dark. When she got back out to the car, she was robbed at knifepoint."

Amber gasped and stepped toward him. "Did she…" Unable to put the thought into words, she let the question trail off.

"It wasn't enough to take her purse. He had to stab her, too. Hit an artery." Caleb's fingers tightened into fists. "While I lay sleeping on the living room couch, my wife bled out in the grocery store parking lot."

Amber closed the last of the distance between them and slid her fingers into his clenched hands. "I'm so sorry, Caleb." Both for what had happened to him and for her outburst of a few moments ago.

He relaxed his grip and allowed her to take his hands. "Do you know how many times I've asked myself why I didn't go?"

"It wasn't your fault." She squeezed his hands and continued, her tone pleading. "Women go to the store alone in the evening all the time without giving it a second thought. You had no way of knowing what would happen."

"But I knew what *could* happen. I'm a cop."

"There are lots things that *could* happen. If we constantly dwelt on those, we'd never leave our homes."

He offered her a weak smile but it was devoid of joy. Her heart twisted. How could she help him when she didn't know how to help herself?

"Your decision resulted in bad consequences, but it was completely innocent. You can't keep beating yourself up."

He looked down at her, brows raised.

"Okay, okay." She gave him a sheepish smile. "Someday I'll figure out how to take my own advice."

In the meantime she'd stay busy. Busy was good. Maybe it wasn't as noble as being spurred by a philanthropic heart. But doing good couldn't be bad, even with the wrong motivation. It was certainly better than trying to numb the pain with alcohol. Like Liv.

Amber followed Caleb to her home's entrance then watched him make his way to his truck. As soon as he climbed into the driver's seat, she closed the door and twisted the lock. The deadbolt swung over with a sturdy click, the sound symbolizing safety and security.

It was a security she didn't feel. Because the killer too often found a way around whatever precautions they'd taken.

She'd told Caleb that all kinds of things could happen. Uncertainty and unpredictability were regular facts of life.

But it wasn't the unpredictable that was hanging over her like a heavy black cloud. It was the predictable.

Ten years ago, a man had lost his life, and she and her friends had each played a part. Now, justice was coming, at least someone's perverted sense of justice.

He'd given them warning. More than once.
Each of them would pay.
It was just a matter of time.

SEVEN

Caleb picked up the remote and punched in two numbers. A herd of elephants replaced the pretty news anchor who'd occupied the screen. He wasn't staying to watch the nature program, but since he didn't like a silent house, he assumed Kira didn't, either. Tess probably didn't have a preference one way or the other.

He laid the remote on the end table and picked up his keys. Kira beat him to the door, tail wagging furiously. He knelt and cupped the dog's face between his hands. "I'm sorry, girl. You have to stay here."

Those big brown eyes couldn't possibly look any sadder. He ruffled the fur on the back of her neck and gave her a couple of pats.

"I'll only be gone for the day." And his friend would be dropping by twice to walk her and feed both her and Tess. Knowing Cortland and his affection for animals, he'd probably hang out for a while to love on them both. "Trust me. I'm leaving you in good hands."

Kira gave a single bark, a final plea to take her with him. He straightened and turned his back on a pouting dog and the soothing voice of the TV program narrator. As he closed the door, an elephant bellowed in the background.

He removed his phone from its case. He'd promised to let Amber know when he was coming in her direction.

Two days ago their friendship had deepened to a new level. He hadn't planned to share those personal details about his wife. But when Amber had accused him of never experiencing regret, he hadn't been able to let it go. Now he was glad he hadn't. Honesty was important in a friendship.

He stopped before opening the truck door and scrolled to her last call. Today they'd celebrate the Fourth at her uncle's ranch in Ocala. According to Amber, they had a big party every year with food and games and even a live band.

Before he had a chance to place the call, the phone vibrated in his hand and a number appeared on the screen. Frank Mason again. Knowing Caleb's acquaintances were involved, Frank was keeping him up to date as events occurred rather than letting him find out when he reported to work.

The call meant something had happened.

Frank skipped the greeting. "As of last night, we had a new development and it's not good. Two people dead."

Caleb's stomach dropped to his knees. *Oh, God, please don't let it be Amber.* "Who?" The word came out in a whisper.

"Raymond Ellis and the deputy who was watching him."

His jaw went lax. "He killed the deputy, too? How?"

"Raymond had a late-afternoon doctor's appointment in Dunnellon. The deputy followed him. They never made it back home. Both vehicles were found wrecked along 40, several miles apart. Numerous shots had been fired into the deputy's vehicle. One hit him in the face."

Caleb closed his eyes. "And Raymond?"

"Shooting wasn't necessary. He was killed on impact. His car slammed into a tree so hard, the engine ended up in the back seat. Based on what we've been able to put together, someone was waiting alongside the road with a high-powered rifle. After Raymond passed, the person stepped out and fired several shots into the deputy's car. Then the subject jumped back into his vehicle and went after Raymond, who apparently tried to flee."

Frank cleared his throat. "Raymond either lost control of the car and ran off the road or he was forced off by the other vehicle."

"What were Logan Cleary's whereabouts?"

"Driving home from work in Chiefland."

Caleb leaned against the door of his truck. Four down, two to go. If not for the dead deputy, Raymond's death could look like an accident. The man's driving record was terrible, with several speeding tickets and a couple of DUIs. In fact, Raymond had just gotten his license back after a five-year suspension.

But this was no accident. Raymond was yet another victim of someone's perverted sense of justice.

One by one, debts are paid.

Ramona, Alex, Vincent and now Raymond. *One by one.*

Amber and Liv had been out in the open all day Monday and the killer hadn't taken a shot at either of them. But that wasn't how he worked. He waited until each of his victims was alone.

As soon as Caleb ended the call, he climbed into his truck and called Amber.

After two rings, her cheery voice came through the phone. "Good morning." She was likely looking forward to a day of fun with family and friends.

He was about to put a damper on her enthusiasm. "I'm on my way. Until I get there, keep your blinds drawn, stay away from the windows and don't open the door for anyone."

"What's going on?" The cheer had turned to concern.

He clamped the phone into the holder on his dash and plugged it into the truck's stereo system. "Raymond's gone, along with the deputy who was watching him."

She gasped. "The deputy was killed, too?"

As he backed from the drive, there was movement on the other end of the line.

"Don't look out the window."

"I want to make sure the deputy is still there."

"He's there, along with backup. Detective Mason assured me that, after last night, they're doubling your protection." Not only were units watching from the road, deputies were also patrolling on foot.

She released a pent-up breath. "Okay. I'll trust they're still standing guard. But be careful. I don't want you to walk into anything."

"I'm watching." He paused. "You mentioned Monday about maybe having Liv stay with you. It might not be a bad idea. Better yet, any chance Hunter and his wife could put you both up?"

"They've got a two-bedroom house and Meagan uses the second one for her studio. It's just got a daybed. Too cozy for two people."

"Convenience isn't a consideration right now. Your focus needs to be on safety—both yours and Liv's."

"I know. I'll make a decision today."

"And the cats?"

"I'm calling now. I won't put it off any longer." Her tone was heavy with resignation.

"Good. If you have to go into hiding, you'll need to be ready to leave at a moment's notice."

He ended the call and made a right onto 24, which would take him the rest of the way to Cedar Key. Staying with Hunter would be better than staying alone. Leaving Cedar Key altogether, would be better yet.

An idea stirred and his pulse quickened. He might know just the place—away from Cedar Key, surrounded by pastureland bordered by woods. It was vacant, owned by his aunt and uncle. Tonight he'd give them a call.

Amber would have to take time off work, something she'd balk at. But it was better than being a sitting duck in Cedar Key.

When he pulled into Amber's driveway, the blinds were drawn. He scanned the area then exited the truck. A car sat at the edge of the road and another one waited on the opposite side two doors down. Both matched the descriptions Frank had given him.

As he closed the truck door, a silver Taurus made its way down the street, a middle-aged blond woman inside. She cast him a sideways glance and raised a hand in greeting. Likely not their killer.

He turned to make his way toward the house. A viburnum hedge stretched across the front, broken only by the small porch. Something white lay at the base of the far right shrub. Maybe a piece of trash. Or something more sinister.

After retrieving some latex gloves from his truck, he stepped closer to inspect what he'd seen. It was paper, crumpled into a tight ball.

He glanced at the woods twenty feet away. Someone approaching from there could wait until the deputies had moved to the other side of the house, lay the object under the bush and disappear in a matter of seconds. Or if they had a half-decent throwing arm, they wouldn't even have to leave the woods.

He picked up the crumpled sheet and carried it to Amber's porch. After ringing the bell, he called a greeting through the front door. The blinds to the right separated then fell into place. Good. She was being extra cautious.

The door swung open and Amber's eyes dipped to his latex-covered hand. "What is that?"

"I'm hoping it's a piece of trash that blew into your yard. It was under one of your shrubs."

After carefully unwrapping what he held, he flattened it against one of her end tables. It was six lines, written in poetry format. A knot of dread formed in his gut before he even read the words.

Amber stepped up next to him and he draped an arm across her shoulder, the supportive action feeling not only natural but necessary. As he scanned the words, he pulled her closer.

Deputies, officers, you've got them in force—
You, your boyfriend and your brother, of course.
That security you feel is just a mirage,
'Cause justice is a bullet you can't dodge.
When I decide your payment is due,
the armies of Heaven won't be able to save you.

Amber looked up at him, her green eyes wide, and a sense of protectiveness surged through him. He'd always fought for the underdog, for those being bullied. It was in his nature, an intricate part of his makeup.

But this was different, the motivation behind his actions more than pity and a simple quest for justice. If he wasn't careful, Amber was going to slip right past his professional exterior and get hold of his heart.

He'd told God that if He chose to send the right woman along, he wouldn't fight it. But it would have to be someone he could keep safe. Falling for a cop wasn't an option.

Amber stepped away and started to pace. "While we were at Atsena Otie, Liv wondered if he was watching us. This proves he was."

"And he was close enough to realize Hunter and I were with you."

"And close enough to all of us to know who you guys are."

She didn't mention the label he'd been given, so he didn't, either.

She stopped pacing, her expression thoughtful. "I'm guessing Logan was nowhere near."

"Chiefland."

"I still think he's somehow involved. It's obvious he's holding a serious grudge. He wouldn't mind seeing every one of us dead. He knows us, he knows you, and it's likely he knows Hunter, being we all grew up in Chiefland."

"Believe me, he's topping the list of suspects."

"He's the *only* suspect."

"True." Only one suspect and no hard evidence against him. Last night, Liv had gone through Amber's yearbook and hadn't been able to give him any more than Amber had.

Caleb indicated the crumpled paper lying on the table. "We need to turn this over to the police."

She gave him a crooked smile. "We *are* the police."

"Someone who's on duty and can do an official report. And we need to get you some safer living accommodations."

She nodded. "I called Sheltering Hands. They'll be placing my four somewhere else."

"Good. And what about Liv?"

"She called this morning. She came down with some kind of flu bug during the night and isn't going anywhere, even told the deputy watching her place that she was making his job easy, taking some heavy-duty medicine and staying in bed. She's pretty free right now. I don't think she has any pets, and I know she doesn't have a job. If I don't move in with Hunter, I'll see if she wants to move in with me."

Amber picked up her purse and walked to the door. "I don't want to think about it right now. Let's give the poem to one of the guys watching this place and get out of here. I want to go to Uncle Randy's and forget about everything."

"Sounds like a plan."

She seemed to be handling everything better than Olivia, but the events of the past two weeks were taking their toll. Dark shadows underlined her eyes and creases of concern often marred her face. She needed a break from the stress and worry and fear, if only for a day.

While she enjoyed herself, he'd remain alert for both of them. Other law enforcement would be watching, first making sure they weren't followed and then standing guard at her uncle's ranch.

But he wouldn't relax his vigilance. Whatever Amber did, he'd be watching.

If anyone wanted to hurt her, they'd have to go through him first.

Amber stood in an open field with a dozen other people. Thirty feet away three wooden circular targets were fastened to posts. Her father was in front of her, to the right. He held a bow in one hand and arrow in his other, pulled back, ready to release.

Archery was an activity he could do. Actually there were several. It was gainful employment that was the issue. When he surprised everybody by pulling through his massive heart attack, continuing his stucco business had been out of the question. Hauling around ladders, scaffolding and buckets of goop weren't on his list of approved activities. So her mom had taken a job as office manager for a large medical facility, and they'd been able to keep the house. Barely.

The familiar knot of guilt formed in her gut. That night, all of their lives had made a complete one-eighty. Although her father had since been approved for disability payments, her mom had never been able to leave the nine-to-five grind.

But through it all, they'd never complained. Or placed guilt. She'd done enough of the latter for all of them.

She shifted her attention to Caleb, several yards to her father's left. He was dressed the way he'd been two days ago, except today's shirt was a deep maroon. He filled it out as well as he had the blue one. Currently he stood with his feet shoulder-width apart, bow drawn, aiming at a board identical to the one in front of her father. Archery was a new activity at this year's Independence Day celebration. She didn't know yet if she was a fan.

Caleb opened his right hand. The arrow sailed through the air and hit the edge of the bull's-eye with a sharp thud, its point embedded deep in the wood.

She handed him a second arrow. "You look like you've done this before."

"I didn't participate on a team, but when I was a kid, my uncle taught me how to use a bow and arrow. I spent a lot of hours doing target practice at his farm."

She arched a brow. "I thought you were all about studies and band and chess."

"I had a few activities that weren't nerdy."

She laughed then handed him the third arrow. While he prepared his shot, she swiped the perspiration from her forehead. Clouds dotted the sky, providing brief periods of respite from the blazing sun. But even in the shade, it was still hot. A heavy rain would drive them all to the huge pole barn for protection, but it would also make the temperatures more tolerable.

A good rain was possible. Today's forecast had been a carbon copy of yesterday's, which had been the same as the day before—partly cloudy with a chance of afternoon thunderstorms.

After his fourth shot, everyone stopped to retrieve arrows. Caleb removed his from the center of the board then handed the bow to Amber. Instead of walking her to the point where he'd taken his shots, he stopped a few feet closer to the target. "Try it from here."

She pulled back the arrow, her arm quivering with the effort. When she released it, it made a sloppy arc, finishing in a nosedive. She frowned at the shaft protruding from the ground at a sharp angle. It had looked much easier when Caleb had done it.

Her second attempt went slightly farther. She heaved a sigh. "I can't believe they used to fight wars with these things."

"You've got to fix your form. May I?"

"Please do."

Caleb moved to stand behind her and gripped her shoulders. "First, you need to turn to the side. You're facing the target too directly."

After he'd rotated her body, he placed his left hand over hers and stepped closer, his chest resting against her shoulder blades.

"Hold the bow steady and draw back, nice and smooth." His right hand wrapped around hers, putting her in the circle of his arms. Her heart fluttered and her palms grew slick. She'd be lying if she attributed it to the heat or the activity with the bow. And she'd be an even bigger liar if she denied that being there somehow felt right.

Caleb seemed oblivious to their closeness. He continued with his lesson, his cheek against the side of her head. "You're bringing your right hand just below your ear." His voice was liquid-smooth, sending a wave of goose bumps cascading over her. "Notice the tension gets tighter and tighter. At a certain point, it's going to get suddenly easier. Check your aim and release."

She did as instructed and the arrow cut a straight path to the target. It didn't make the bull's-eye, but it hit the board.

She spun in his arms then stopped, her face inches from his. "We did it."

His jaw tightened almost imperceptibly. He released her and cleared his throat. "Good job. Now try it without any help."

She seated the arrow and drew it back, focusing on her form. When she released it, the arrow missed the target by a good six feet and disappeared into the edge of the woods.

"Not bad."

She cocked a brow at him and he shrugged.

"It went a long way. Your aim is just a little off."

"A little off? If that round board out there was the broad side of a barn, I would've still missed."

"It takes practice."

"I'd better stick with my pistol."

She handed Caleb her bow and walked toward the target, picking up the first two arrows on the way. While Caleb pulled the third from the wooden board, she marched toward the woods.

In the shade of the trees, the temperature felt ten degrees cooler. A soft breeze rustled the leaves, creating a steady *shhhh*. She turned in a slow circle and wasn't surprised to see Caleb had followed her. She spread her arms, palms up. "I was sure it went into the woods right here."

"Maybe it went farther than you realized."

She moved deeper into the trees and searched until she was sure she'd covered every square inch of ground.

Finally she heaved a sigh. "I can't believe I've got to tell Uncle Randy I lost one of his new arrows."

"I'm sure he'll forgive you."

While Caleb spoke, a rustle sounded nearby and she stiffened, her right hand going for the weapon hidden under her shirt. "Do you hear that?" Her words were barely above a whisper.

Caleb stood stock-still. "I don't hear anything except the wind." His tone matched hers.

"I thought I heard someone moving through the woods." She lowered her hand but the tension lingered. "I'm hearing things."

She had to be. As she'd driven over, Caleb had constantly surveyed their surroundings, the two deputies some distance behind. No one knew where she was—at least no one who would communicate her whereabouts to the killer.

She shook off the uneasiness. She'd heard the wind and her stressed-out mind had turned it into something more.

When they exited the woods, Uncle Randy was walking toward the archery area.

"Archery competition at one o'clock." He looked at his watch. "One hour to get yourself warmed up."

She handed her bow and the arrows she'd collected to her cousin Mark and headed toward her uncle.

He watched them approach, a friendly smile spreading across his face. "I hope you young'uns are enjoying yourselves." Raised in Alabama, he spoke with a slow drawl and had that Southern gentleman charm down to a T.

Amber returned his smile. "We are. But I think I'll pass on the archery competition. The three-legged race is more my speed."

"Your aunt Louise is getting people together right now in the field east of the barn. You know where it is."

Yes, she did. Though Uncle Randy had added other events over the years, the three-legged race had been part of the games for as long as she could remember, along with corn hole and lawn bowling.

As she made her way toward the barn, Caleb grinned. "I haven't been called a young'un in about fifteen years."

"To Uncle Randy, anyone born after 1970 is a young'un." Husband to her dad's elder sister, he was a good decade and a half older than her parents. But he wasn't likely to slow down anytime soon. Acres of fields lay harvested and plowed, ready for next month's planting, and he'd added several cows to the couple dozen grazing the pastures.

When they reached the barn, Aunt Louise was passing out large bandannas. A whistle hung on a cord around her neck and several ribbons with medals were draped over one arm. Six or eight couples already had their bandannas secured and were practicing walking, Hunter and Meagan included. At the other end of the field a group of scrub oaks stood draped in Spanish moss, an orange finish line sprayed on the grass in front of them.

Aunt Louise held up a bandanna. "Are you kids going to play?"

Amber hurried forward to take what she held. Five minutes ago, they were young'uns. Now they were kids. She thanked her aunt and moved to where Caleb waited at the start line.

After rolling up the scarf, she tied her right leg to Caleb's left. "This is something I'm good at. The secret is setting up a rhythm."

She straightened and slid an arm around his waist. "Hold me tight. We have to work as a single unit." After Caleb wrapped his arm around her shoulders, she continued. "We'll start with the tied legs and count one-two-one-two, gradually picking up speed."

When everyone was in place, Aunt Louise blew the whistle. Caleb immediately adjusted his stride to match her shorter one and they fell into an easy rhythm. A few yards from the orange line, Caleb cast a glance over her shoulder.

"Your brother's catching up."

She groaned. "Not again."

They pushed for a little more speed and lost the rhythm as they crossed the finish line. Amber stumbled and only Caleb's tight hold kept her from falling. Once she'd fully regained her balance, he released her and she removed the tie. When she'd finished, Aunt Louise stood in front of her.

"First place in the three-legged race. Congratulations." A red, white and blue ribbon went around Amber's neck, the gold medal hanging right below her chest. Aunt Louise presented a matching one to Caleb and selected silver ones for Hunter and Meagan.

Amber held up her medal. "Whoever collects the most of these by the end of the day wins."

"What do we win?"

"Absolutely nothing." She grinned. "A few years ago, Aunt Louise ordered about five hundred of them from a discount party supply place. For each game, a medal is awarded for first, second and third place." She dropped the medal to let it dangle from its ribbon. "What do you say we grab some of that picnic lunch spread out in the pole barn?"

"Sounds good. I need my nourishment for the archery tournament coming up."

When they'd finished eating, they joined eight or ten other people in the field. Two held bows.

Uncle Randy addressed the group. "We're missing the third bow. I think someone's trying to play Robin Hood and walked off with it over his shoulder."

Some chuckles went through the group but Amber's chest tightened. Her arrow and now the bow. The rustle she'd heard in the woods. Had someone taken her arrow and waited until everyone had left the area to steal a bow?

As she studied the trees beyond the targets, the fine hairs on the back of her neck stood up. Surely someone wouldn't be bold enough to take a shot at her with people all around.

Besides her family and Caleb, one deputy was watching her vehicle and another had been close by ever since she'd arrived.

She shifted her gaze to her uncle, who was providing instructions to the contestants. Everyone would get three shots. The three people who came closest to the center of the bull's-eye would square off against one another.

After forming two lines, the first contestants stepped forward and took aim. Within a few minutes Uncle Randy announced the three finalists. Caleb would be competing against her father and her cousin Mark.

Caleb stepped forward, took aim at the far left target and released. The arrow hit the board less than an inch right of center.

Next up was her father. He was good, likely equal to Caleb. He'd taken up the hobby a year ago, bought a bow and installed a target near his rear fence. It was probably his prodding that had convinced Uncle Randy to add archery to their July Fourth activities.

Her father released his arrow. A second later its point was embedded in the wood just left of center. Unless Mark's shot was perfect, this one would have to be decided with a ruler.

Caleb handed his bow to her cousin, who positioned himself in front of the third target.

His arrow also made the bull's-eye, but wasn't as close to center as the other two.

Uncle Randy moved forward to inspect both targets. He didn't have a ruler, but he made due with his fingers, using his pinkie as a guide. After moving back and forth between the targets, he stopped at one and held up a hand. "This one's closer by a quarter of a finger's width."

Caleb sighed, but his smile said he was enjoying himself too much to feel any real disappointment.

"I lost to your father."

"That's okay. As long as we don't lose to Hunter. Competition's always fiercer between siblings."

Uncle Randy draped a ribbon around Caleb's neck. A silver second-place medal hung from it. Mark approached wearing a bronze one, and after Amber gave him a high-five, he pulled her into a hug. Aunt Louise and Uncle Randy's youngest, he was the same age as Hunter and had always been like another big brother.

By the time Mark released her, her father was standing next to him. She smiled up at him and wrapped both arms around his neck. "First place. Congratulations, Daddy."

"Thank you, sweetheart." His hold on her tightened. Her father hugged like he meant it, the gesture always filled with love and acceptance. Even when she'd been at her worst, and discipline was involved, she'd never doubted his love.

When she stepped away, Caleb was grinning. "So the winners get a medal *and* a hug?"

She gave him a teasing smile. "Congratulations on your incredible performance out there."

She looped her arms around his neck and his came up to circle her back. A few seconds later he gave her a couple of rough pats and released her. A sudden awkwardness hung between them. The awkwardness was likely just on her end.

Her dad spared her any further discomfort. He extended his hand to Caleb. "Congratulations. It was almost a tie."

Caleb accepted the handshake and her dad patted his shoulder with the other hand. "I'm glad you could come today. Amber mentioned you're a detective and you've been working on a case together."

She cast a sideways glance at Caleb. She'd warned him on the way over that her parents didn't know about the attempts on her life. As far as her father knew, the deputy hanging close was a coworker of Caleb's there to enjoy the activities. Reducing his stress sometimes meant keeping things from him.

Caleb nodded. "Yes, we have."

"Take good care of my little girl."

"I plan to."

Amber stifled a groan and let it escape as soon as her father was out of earshot. At least he hadn't given Caleb *the talk*. Of course, she was ten years older now. Besides, Caleb wasn't a date. If he was, her father would probably approve and find the talk unnecessary.

As Amber headed toward other activities, her skin pickled again with a sense of being watched. She cast a glance at the woods and stiffened. Had there been movement? Or was she imagining things?

"Are you okay?" Caleb's brow was creased in concern.

"I'm wondering what happened to my arrow and the other bow."

"I've been thinking the same thing."

She tried to shake off the uneasiness. "No one knows I'm here."

"We weren't followed." Caleb's tone reflected her own doubts.

As she moved farther from the archery field, her uneasiness gradually dissipated. She and Caleb participated in more games and, by the time they sat down to dinner, they'd each collected several more medals.

After filling up on ribs, baked beans and garlic bread, Amber and Caleb headed to the archery field with several others.

Caleb leaned toward her as they walked. "This gives me another opportunity to try to beat your dad."

Her father turned and grinned at him. "I heard that. You sure you've got it in you?"

As they lined up for their shots, the banter continued, the sense of competition as high as it'd been when there were medals at stake.

When they'd finished the first round, Caleb moved forward with Amber's dad and cousin Mark. Amber followed and stood beside one of the targets while they compared their best shots and declared Caleb that round's champion.

He gave her a fist pump, and she laughed. It was fun seeing him have such a great time. She leaned against the painted board and smiled at him. "Congratulations."

Something whistled through the air behind her, and a fraction of a second later, an arrow hit the back of the board inches from her arm. She gasped and whirled around.

Mark and two others ran past her toward the woods. Caleb stopped long enough to make sure she was unharmed before following the other three. When she turned around, the deputy was running toward her, speaking into his radio. He'd been standing some distance behind her and to the side.

She ran with him into the woods. Caleb wouldn't be thrilled with her decision, but only he and the deputy were armed. A little extra firepower wouldn't hurt.

"Here's the bow." Caleb's comment carried to her from a short distance ahead. "No one touch it."

She stopped and listened. With so many people looking for the killer, there was rustling all around her. She moved forward, pistol drawn.

A few minutes later, an engine roared to life. Her heart pounded. That sound hadn't come from where they'd all parked. She made a sharp right and took off.

A minute later, she broke through the tree line and skidded to a stop at a fence. Ahead of her, a packed dirt road separated two fields. A thunderstorm had come through around four o'clock and released all its fury over the course of twenty minutes. While everyone had waited under the protection of the pole barn, the downpour had turned the freshly plowed ground to mud.

Caleb stopped next to her and the others joined them.

Amber pointed. "Look."

On the other side of the fence, a vehicle had slung mud in a fan-shaped spray, then fishtailed for several yards before gaining enough traction to make it down the dirt drive. The wide metal gate at the end was open. But whoever had left the erratic trail was gone.

Mark stepped up next to her. "What's going on?"

When she looked at her cousin, her father was approaching from behind him. His gait was stiff, his jaw tight. "That's what I want to know."

As soon as he reached her, she put a hand on his arm. "You shouldn't have run out here."

"You think I'm going to stay behind when someone's shooting arrows at my little girl?"

She stifled another groan. When she'd announced her intention to pursue a career in law enforcement, her father hadn't been pleased. His only consolation had been that she'd planned to try to land a job with Cedar Key. Not only was it a small, safe town, her dad had envisioned Hunter always being nearby to keep her safe.

Before she could form a response, Caleb stepped to her aid. "Whether it was a prank or some kind of warning for one of us, we should probably get going."

She nodded. They'd planned to make their excuses and leave before dark anyway. As they headed back the way they'd come, she cast a glance at her father. He was smart enough to know something was up. But at least Caleb had bought her some time to formulate an explanation.

After brief goodbyes to her uncle and the others, she hurried to the RAV4 with Caleb. He insisted on driving. She didn't argue.

As soon as she'd settled herself in the passenger seat, she closed her eyes and let her head fall against the headrest, suddenly exhausted. When they were on their way, she pivoted her head to the left and opened her eyes. "Thanks for coming with me."

"Thanks for inviting me." He grinned over at her. "Or I should say thanks for not fighting your brother when *he* invited me."

Until thirty minutes ago, it had been a good day. Her aunt and uncle's Independence Day bash was always fun. Spending it with Caleb had made it even better. She couldn't deny the physical attraction between them. But it was more than that. Caleb almost made her feel whole again. There was something soothing about his presence. He exuded a calm peace that she'd lacked for most of her life. If she could spend more time with him...

No, it wouldn't be fair to Caleb. She didn't do relationships. She didn't have the time.

"So what are we missing?" His question penetrated her thoughts.

"A couple hours of shooting the breeze and telling stories, seeing who can top the others. Then fireworks."

"Uh-oh, would we have had to arrest someone if we'd stayed?"

She smiled. "My uncle's stash consists of sparklers, firecrackers and glow worms—the legal stuff. I can't vouch for what my cousins and their friends bring."

"Maybe it's best we're not there to witness it."

He turned onto Highway 316, and she stared through the windshield. Ahead and to the left, the sun was sitting low in the sky, staining it shades of pink and lavender. By the time they got to Cedar Key, it would be dark.

She glanced again at Caleb. He seemed to be avoiding discussing what had happened. Or maybe he was waiting until she was ready.

"How did he find me?"

Caleb frowned, his brows drawing together. "I don't know."

"I didn't tell anyone except Liv and Hunter where I was going. And I talked about it during a phone conversation with my mom."

"Someone apparently overheard."

"Any chance my house is bugged?" Just the thought made her feel violated.

"We'll definitely have it checked out."

It was the only thing that made sense. The killer wasn't omnipresent. And he couldn't read minds.

But he'd somehow known where to find her, taken a shot and slipped away without being seen.

What kind of enemy were they dealing with?

EIGHT

Caleb turned onto Noble Avenue and cast a glance over at Amber. This morning's trip to Williston had taken place under a brilliant blue sky. But Amber's face didn't reflect the cheeriness outside. She looked to be on the verge of tears.

He covered her hand with his. "They'll be all right."

She gave a couple quick bobs of her head but didn't speak.

"It's temporary." Hopefully "temporary" wouldn't stretch into weeks. Law enforcement had gotten the warrant they'd requested to search Logan's home and turned up nothing. Monitoring his cell phone and emails hadn't given them anything of worth, either.

Caleb braked at a traffic light and squeezed Amber's hand. "If the cats haven't found permanent homes by the time this is over, you can take them again."

"I know." Her smile was equal parts appreciation and sadness. "I feel like I'm abandoning them. Did you see how sad they looked?"

"They'll get over it. Think how happy they'll be when you come for them."

He released her hand and stepped on the gas. He was driving Amber's RAV4. She'd ridden in the back all the way over, a carrier holding two cats on each side of her. She'd taken turns consoling them, her voice soft and soothing against a backdrop of caterwauling.

At least the return trip to Cedar Key would be quiet. Too quiet. If only he could think of a way to lift her spirits.

Amber's ringtone sounded and she pulled her phone from her purse. Maybe the caller would be able to do what he couldn't.

She sighed and swiped the screen. "Hey, Liv."

Okay, maybe not.

According to Amber, Liv had phoned first thing this morning and Amber had talked with her during breakfast. A second call came shortly after he'd arrived and they were loading up the cats. Now a third.

Liv wasn't just high maintenance. She was a poster child for needy friends. Probably not the best thing for Amber's state of mind.

She set her purse on the floor at her feet. "I'm

not busy. Caleb and I are heading back from Williston. Then I'm moving in with Hunter and Meagan." She paused. "You should do the same—go stay with friends or family, only until this is over. You shouldn't be alone."

As Amber talked, he couldn't help but smile. She was using the same soothing tone she'd used with the cats. The sympathetic nature she possessed came with an infinite well of patience.

By the time Amber finished with Liv, they'd already crossed the first bridge into Cedar Key. She slid her phone into her purse. "If Hunter and Meagan had room, I'd ask Liv to come and stay with us."

"What about her parents?"

"Her mom's remarried and living in North Carolina. Her stepdad doesn't want anything to do with her." She sighed. "That's been the story of her life."

His heart twisted. With a loving, supportive family of his own, it was hard to imagine Olivia's life.

"What about friends? She must have someone who would put her up temporarily."

"According to Liv, she doesn't. She said she asked a girl she used to work with, but she's newly married and her husband won't take in strays."

At his quick glance, she frowned. "Those

were Liv's words. Another friend lives in an efficiency apartment and doesn't have the room. She left a message for a third, who never returned her call. I got the impression these were more acquaintances than friends."

He shook his head. No family and no friends close enough to count on in an emergency.

When he pulled into Amber's driveway, she opened the passenger door. "Thanks for going with me. If I'd had to do this alone, I'd have been a blubbering idiot."

"What are friends for?"

He stepped from the truck. *Friends*. That was what they were. And he'd keep reminding himself of that as often as he needed to.

The problem was, the hug at her uncle's place yesterday had almost done him in. He'd been teasing when he'd asked. He hadn't expected it to affect him the way it had.

Everything lately reminded him of how lonely he was. The past four years he'd had no problem convincing himself that love wasn't worth the risk of loss that came with it. Unfortunately his heart was no longer listening to reason. The TV programs playing in the background, the concern of friends and the love he received from his family were poor substitutes for the intimacy and companionship he'd shared with his wife.

After climbing from the vehicle, Amber walked to the road to retrieve her mail. As she flipped through what she held, her brows drew together. "One of these is handwritten, no return address."

He looked down at jagged block lettering now disturbingly familiar. "According to the postmark, this was mailed two days ago from Bronson."

Amber pursed her lips. "Considering Bronson's where Liv is, I'd rather *not* mention that part to her. She's freaked out enough as it is."

"Let me get some latex gloves." They hadn't gotten one viable print from the other pieces of paper, but he'd never stop hoping the killer would eventually get careless.

Once inside the house, he opened the envelope and carefully removed its contents—a single page folded in thirds. As expected, it was another poem. He held it where she could read along with him.

Night is coming, the end is near.
The death knell is pealing. Can you hear?
Four have paid, only two remain.
Both girls equally bear the blame.
Ten years has passed, but we won't forgive.
Who is next, Amber or Liv?

His chest tightened. Amber looked up at him, her eyes wide, and he resisted the urge to pull her into his arms.

"How soon can you be ready to go?" The tension inside came out in his tone. "The sooner we get you to Hunter's, the better."

"I'm ready now. I got packed before you arrived this morning, except for Tippy's litter box."

"I'll help you get loaded. Then I'll follow you. We can take this with us and call the police when we get there."

"Or we can give it to the deputy again, let him add it to the other evidence. He's probably bored out there anyway."

She disappeared down the hall and returned wheeling two suitcases, one large, the other carry-on size.

Soon, Caleb had loaded both, along with the litter box and a bag of cat supplies, into the bed of his truck. After putting the cat carrier into the RAV4, Amber backed from the drive and pulled onto the street, with Caleb following close behind.

Once he'd unloaded everything and Amber had locked Tippy in Meagan's studio, Caleb turned to leave.

Hunter held up a hand. "How about joining

us for lunch? Meagan has had chili simmering most of the morning. It's almost ready."

Yeah, the aromas emanating from the kitchen had been driving him crazy since he arrived. "If it tastes half as good as it smells, I can't resist."

Hunter invited them to sit in the living room. Meagan had given a brief greeting when they'd arrived, then returned to work on a painting she'd been commissioned to do.

A muffled woof sounded from down the hall and Hunter moved in that direction. A few moments later a chocolate Lab bounded into the room ahead of him. The dog went straight to Amber and tried to slather her face with sloppy kisses. His tail beat side to side at a rapid pace.

Amber laughed, holding him back. "This is Bruno."

"He adores you."

"He adores everybody. Get ready, because you're next."

As promised, Bruno moved to the other body on the couch, not the least concerned about his status as stranger. Two big paws landed in Caleb's lap and a wet tongue slid across his jaw before he could react. Caleb cupped the dog's cheeks and scratched his neck.

Hunter made a hand signal. "Bruno, come. Sit." He gave an apologetic smile as he set-

tled into his recliner. "He's obnoxiously sweet."
Hunter grew serious. "I'm glad you finally talked some sense into my bullheaded sister."

The warmth behind the words belied their sternness. Caleb had always liked Hunter. But with the five-year age difference, they'd never been close. Now it was no big deal.

"I'm glad, too. I'll be resting a lot easier." A seed of doubt crept in. "I'm just concerned about during the day, when she's not with you."

"I'll keep an eye on her then, too. It helps that we work together. Sunday, I plan to take her to church with me, even if I have to drag her there kicking and screaming. You're welcome to join us if you'd like."

"I think I'll do that."

Amber frowned at him. "Don't you have a Sunday school class to teach?"

"Not now. I team teach with another guy. We trade off every quarter. July, August and September are his months."

"You two are ganging up on me."

Hunter shrugged. "Whatever works."

Caleb settled into the couch, a sense of peace washing over him. Hunter wouldn't only care for her physical well-being. He'd be every bit as concerned with her spiritual condition.

Over the past three weeks Amber had been swept into an unthinkable nightmare.

But God worked in mysterious ways.

Maybe here with Hunter and Meagan was exactly where she needed to be.

Amber stood clutching the pew in front of her, Caleb to her left. Hunter stood on her right, Meagan on his other side. All around her, music swelled as people lifted their voices in praise. She mouthed the words, her voice a mere whisper. Participating in worship seemed hypocritical of her. She didn't belong here.

It had nothing to do with the people. She knew most of them. Cedar Key was small, and she'd lived here long enough to be well acquainted with eighty percent of the full-time population and a good number of the regular visitors. So those in attendance weren't making her uncomfortable.

It was the place. Cold and sterile and far too holy.

Hunter shouldn't have insisted she come. He'd used the excuse that he didn't want to leave her alone. She didn't buy it. With the house securely locked, a guard dog inside and two deputies outside, no one was going to get to her.

No, his insistence was another example of him trying to tell her what to do, the same as he always had. He thought he knew what was best for her.

As the last strains of the final song faded to silence, she took a seat with the rest of the congregation. The screen that had held song lyrics now displayed the sermon title. Scripture verses followed, a passage about King David.

As a child, she'd liked the Bible stories. As a teen, she'd grown bored with them. As an adult, she failed to see their relevance.

The pastor began to read and she half listened, her attention split between his words and her troubled thoughts. Once church was over, they'd head home to enjoy a lunch of roast beef, potatoes and carrots cooked in the Crock-Pot.

And someone would be watching.

With so many people around her, he wouldn't act. But he'd be nearby, waiting for the others to let down their guard and leave her unprotected long enough for him to strike.

Or maybe Liv was his target today. Wherever she was, it wasn't church. She was probably holed up at home, jumping over every sound.

Sadness pressed down on Amber. Here she was, safe and secure under Hunter's and Caleb's protection, and Liv had no one. Levy County was guarding them both. But nothing took the place of the support of family and friends.

Her attention slipped back to the pastor's

words. This wasn't the story of David and Goliath. It was the account of David taking Bathsheba. Amber was familiar with that story, too. Although her Sunday school teachers had likely glossed over some of the details.

Her mind drifted again. Focusing was difficult, not that she was trying very hard. She had too many worries.

Paramount in her thoughts was concern for her cats. Not all of them. Tippy was fine. When Amber had first turned her loose in Meagan's studio, she'd prowled around the room, exploring every nook and cranny. Then she'd curled up in the center of the daybed and taken a nap. Last night the two of them had shared the cramped space.

The other four wouldn't be doing as well. The image of sad eyes set in furry faces still haunted her. When she'd first brought them home, it had taken them almost a month to get comfortable. Now they'd been uprooted again. They were probably scared to death, wondering why she'd abandoned them. Were the repercussions of her actions ten years ago ever going to stop?

The pastor's words cut into her thoughts. God had called David a man after his own heart. *I bet he never got that title back again.*

He'd heaped guilt on top of guilt. First, he'd

slept with a married woman. Then when she'd ended up pregnant, he'd tried to hide what he'd done by calling her husband home from the battlefield. When that hadn't worked, he'd arranged to have the man killed.

Talk about bad choices. At least when she'd texted the invitation to Landon, she hadn't intended any harm. And afterward, when she'd kept Liv's rape a secret, she hadn't hurt anyone. Well, ultimately she had, but it hadn't been intentional. And nothing she'd done had been intended to hurt her father.

But David was a character she could relate to. She knew all about mistakes, and she'd experienced her fair share of guilt. She cast a sideways glance at her brother. Had Hunter spoken with the pastor and gotten him to preach a sermon directed at her?

Or was God trying to get her attention?

She pulled her lower lip between her teeth and fiddled with her bulletin, rolling each of the corners inward.

The pastor read the next passage, where the prophet Nathan called David out on everything he'd done. The king had taken the words to heart. His prayer for forgiveness was displayed on the screen, verses from Psalm 51.

After all he'd done, his relationship with God had been restored. He'd still had to suffer the consequences of his actions, but the guilt had been wiped away.

A spark of hope flickered. Was the same possible for her? Might peace be within her reach?

Notes on the piano sounded and the people stood to sing. This time she didn't even mouth the lyrics. The pastor's persuasive words urged her to the altar while her doubts held her rooted in place. She closed her eyes, a sense of claustrophobia gripping her. She needed sunshine and fresh air.

Pressure against the side of her arm startled her. Caleb leaned close to whisper in her ear. "If you want to go forward, I'll go with you."

She shook her head. She wasn't ready. She might never be ready. How could she let go of ten years of guilt? Especially with reminders of the past all around her?

He laid his hand over hers and squeezed. She'd turned down his request, but he was still offering support. Caleb would make the ideal mate for someone someday. Unfortunately *someday* seemed to be a distant, unreachable point in the future. And *someone* would never be her.

When she opened her eyes, two women and a man knelt at the altar, and a shadow fell across her mind, the fear she'd passed up a one-time opportunity.

Soon people began to file out. She moved

into the aisle and Caleb fell into step beside her. Outside, the sunshine she'd longed for was filtered through a layer of heavy gray clouds. A rain-scented breeze blew, whipping her hair into her face. She tucked it behind one ear, thoughts still on the sermon. "He makes it sound so easy."

"People make it too hard. They think they have to earn God's forgiveness. But that's not how it works. There's no giant scale up there. God isn't going to put all your good deeds on one side and everything bad you've ever done on the other."

Yeah, she knew that, at least with her head. But did she believe it with her heart?

Meagan and Hunter exited the church and when they all piled into Meagan's car, it was starting to sprinkle. By the time they stepped onto the porch, the sky had opened up. But inside was safe and dry. And full of pleasant aromas.

Before Hunter had even closed the door, Bruno bounded into the room from the back of the house, tail wagging. Beginning with Meagan, he worked his way through the group, greeting each of them with equal enthusiasm. Whether left alone for ten minutes or a half day, he could hardly contain himself once he had company again.

Amber walked down the hall to check on the other four-legged resident of the house. Tippy would be happy to see her but wouldn't be nearly as expressive about it as Bruno had been.

As soon as she opened the door, a variety of scents surrounded her—paints, thinners, the roast sending its aroma throughout the house and…something else. Like peanut butter.

But that was impossible. Hunter and Meagan wouldn't allow any products containing peanuts past the front door. Some odd combination of art supply scents had to be tricking her nose.

She moved to where Tippy sat on Meagan's stool, tall and alert. Amber gave her several strokes, then pulled a pair of jeans and T-shirt from the chest of drawers.

After trading the dress for more casual clothes, she waved her hand in front of her nose. The peanut butter smell was faint, but it seemed to permeate her sinuses. She'd always found the odor offensive, maybe because it could kill her.

When she returned to the front of the house, Meagan had already changed clothes and was setting the table. Hunter was sitting on the couch keeping Bruno from being underfoot in the kitchen, and Caleb was keeping him company.

Hunter looked up when she entered the room. "Everything okay? You seem tense."

She shook her head. "If I didn't know better, I'd think Meagan switched to peanut butter based paints."

"What?" Hunter pushed himself to his feet without waiting for an answer.

By the time they reached the end of the hall, both Caleb and Meagan had joined them. Amber entered after the others were inside and closed the door behind them. "What do you smell?"

Hunter looked around the room, and she followed his gaze. Nothing was out of place. If it had been, she'd have noticed.

"All the usual art-related odors." Hunter's nose twitched. "But there's definitely a faint smell of peanut butter.

Meagan nodded. "I agree. And I can promise you, that one has nothing to do with me."

After sniffing the air a couple more times, Hunter opened the blinds.

Amber gasped. The window was closed, but someone had put a softball-sized hole in the glass above the lock.

Caleb yanked the bedspread back. Everything looked the same as when she'd made the bed that morning. But when he turned the pillow over, a light brown smear marked its underside. The same gooey substance coated a two-inch by four-inch section of the sheet.

"Get out of here." Hunter's tone was commanding, not allowing any argument. She didn't plan to give any. But she couldn't get her feet moving. While the deputy had waited outside the church, someone had come into Hunter's house and booby-trapped her temporary bedroom. Someone who knew about her peanut allergy.

She shook her head and gripped the doorknob. As Caleb and Meagan followed her down the hall, Hunter's voice drifted to her from behind the closed bedroom door. He was already on the phone with 911 dispatch.

Amber sank onto the couch, flanked by Caleb on one side and Meagan on the other. "We've been saying all along that the killer is someone who knows us. This is more proof."

Meagan put her hand over Amber's. "Do many people know about your peanut allergy?"

Amber gave her a wry smile. "Only the entire school. I was the one blamed for getting anything containing peanuts banned from school property."

Meagan frowned. "That doesn't give us a very workable number of suspects."

Within minutes, a Cedar Key officer arrived. She'd just finished answering his questions when her cell phone rang. The muscles in her neck tightened. She could guess who was calling without even looking at the screen. She pulled the phone from her purse and confirmed what she already knew.

Liv ignored her greeting and launched into a high-pitched flow of words.

"Liv, slow down."

"He called me." The words were only slightly clearer. "He has my number."

"Where are you?"

"Headed to Cedar Key."

"Is the deputy following you?"

"Yes." A sound came through the phone, half sob, half hiccup. "Can I come over?"

She glanced at Hunter, then Meagan. What could she say? "Sure."

After giving her the address, she hung up the phone. "The killer called Liv's cell phone. She was hysterical. She asked if she could come over." She looked up at Hunter, her brows drawn together in apology. "I hope it's okay."

Hunter pulled her to his side in a brotherly hug. "It'll do her good to spend the afternoon here. And I think Meagan would agree."

Meagan nodded. "Absolutely."

The couple headed into the kitchen to get dinner on the table. A few minutes later the bell rang. When Amber swung open the door, Liv stood on the porch, her face streaked with tears. She threw both arms around Amber's neck. "Thank you for letting me come."

Once Liv released her, Amber led her into the living room. Liv sat on the couch, her phone clutched in one hand. "I got a call from a blocked number."

Liv angled the phone toward Amber. The call log was displayed. Amber's number was listed several times. The call right before the last one read Blocked.

"He said he's watching me, whispered it in a gravelly voice. He said he's going to take out the deputies, then come after me."

Caleb sat in Hunter's recliner and Amber sank down next to Liv. "Did the voice sound familiar?"

"I think it might have been Logan."

Bruno wandered into the room and sat at Caleb's feet, wary eyes locked on Liv. Liv's face lit up. "Aw, this is Hunter's chocolate Lab you told me about." After patting her leg, she stretched out her arm. "Come here, boy."

Bruno sat unflinching. His tail was even still, a rare occurrence. Once Liv calmed down, he'd warm up to her. Bruno loved people. It was cats he had a problem with.

Meagan announced dinner was ready and Liv raised a brow. "I wasn't intending to invite myself to eat here."

Amber stood and motioned for her to follow. "It's okay. There's a whole Crock-Pot full."

The five of them sat around the dining room table, and Bruno plopped down in the corner, his big head resting on his front paws.

As soon as Hunter had blessed the food, Liv put a large bite of roast beef in her mouth and closed her eyes. "This is wonderful."

She ate everything on her plate and took seconds. Hunter had been right. Spending the afternoon with them was good for her.

After sopping up the last drop of gravy with her bread, Liv released a contented sigh. "That totally hit the spot. I haven't eaten like this in forever."

Meagan smiled. "It's nice to have you."

Actually, it *had* been nice. The agitation Liv had shown when she'd first arrived had completely disappeared, and dinner conversation had been pleasant. Of course, she'd been too busy eating to do much talking.

Liv pushed her chair back and stood. "Can you tell me where your restroom is?"

Meagan pointed. "Down the hall. First door on the left."

When Liv walked from the room, Bruno followed at a distance. Amber stood to help clear off the table. Halfway to the kitchen, frenzied barking stopped her in her tracks. She spun as

Tippy rounded the corner, Bruno right behind her. Large jaws clamped down on the cat's tail and she let out an ear-piercing screech.

Amber screamed and the plates she held crashed to the floor. Hunter shot up from the table and dove for Bruno. While he restrained the dog, Amber chased a terrified cat through the house. Meanwhile, Liv stood in the open doorway of the dining room, eyes wide and hands pressed to her mouth.

Tippy finally flew back into the spare bedroom, a beige, brown and white streak. Amber followed her in, closing the door behind her and dropped to her knees. The cat was hunched in the corner, under the daybed.

Amber crawled closer and Tippy hissed. It took several minutes of coaxing before she was able to pull the cat from her hiding place without having her hands and arms shredded.

A couple of soft knocks preceded Hunter's words. "Is Tippy okay?"

Amber laid the cat on the daybed and swiped a hand down her back, finishing with her tail. When she turned her hand over, a brownish-red streak marked her index finger. Bruno had drawn blood. It probably wasn't bad enough to require a vet visit. But what if Tippy got out again?

She stalked across the room and spoke without opening the door. "Where is Bruno?"

"Closed up in our room."

She stepped into the hall. "This was a mistake. I'm taking Tippy home."

Before Hunter could respond, Liv hurried toward her. Tears had pooled on her lower lashes and her face was crumpled. "I'm so sorry. That was the last door on the left. What did I do wrong?"

Amber sighed. She couldn't be angry with Liv. It was an honest mistake. "The bathroom is the *first* door on the left." She pointed at the closed door nearby.

Liv gasped. "I misunderstood. Is the cat okay?"

"I think so. But next time she might not be. I'm going home."

Hunter put a hand on her shoulder. "We've been through this. It's not safe."

"I'm not going to have my cat killed if she gets out again. Law enforcement can guard me as well at my home as they can yours. And if Liv stays with me, they can combine resources. Neither of us will be alone." She blurted out the words before she could change her mind, then turned to Liv. "Are you okay with this?"

A slow smile spread across Liv's face. "I would love to stay with you."

Both Hunter and Caleb offered a few more arguments. She turned away and stalked to the bedroom. Within five minutes she'd be packed. Five minutes after that, she'd have everything loaded. Soon she'd be home, surrounded by her own things.

Moving in with Hunter and Meagan had been a mistake. It had lasted all of seventy-two hours.

Now she was moving back home. With Liv.

She only hoped she wasn't making an even bigger mistake.

NINE

Moonlight slanted through the trees overhead and a damp mist rose from the forest floor. A heavy cloak of silence draped the landscape.

Amber crept through the woods, her feet sinking into the dead leaves with a soft, rhythmic crunch. Her scalp prickled with the sense that someone was watching.

"Hunter?" More silence. "Bobby? Gary?"

The other officers weren't with her, either. Where was her backup?

She reached for her weapon and clutched a handful of fabric. Her shirt. She didn't even have her holster.

Alone and unarmed? What had she been thinking?

Footsteps sounded in the distance and drew closer. She increased her pace from a walk to a jog to a full-out run.

But whoever pursued her continued to gain on her. The heavy tread pounded right behind her and massive hands clamped down on her shoulders, wrenching a terrified scream from her throat—

Her eyes flew open and she jerked in several jagged breaths. She was in her room. Red numerals glowed from the clock on her bedside stand and her comforter was bunched up around her feet. Tippy was gone.

Another scream rent the silence. It didn't come from her. Maybe the other one hadn't, either. Who... Liv!

She snatched her weapon from under the spare pillow and bolted from the bed, the last remnants of sleep banished from her mind. Outside Liv's closed door, she hesitated. Another scream came from inside the room and she twisted the knob with her left hand, weapon ready.

She inched open the door. A beam of moonlight slanted across the bed, illuminating Liv's contorted face. Amber released a pent-up breath. Liv was alone, the only threat in her dreams.

Amber flipped on the light and laid her weapon on the dresser. With Liv's thrashing, she'd trapped almost her entire body in the twisted sheets. Only her right arm was free, her hand clenched into a white-knuckled fist.

"Liv, wake up."

In response Liv released another scream, its shrillness shredding Amber's nerves.

Amber approached the bed and spoke louder. "Olivia, it's a dream. Wake up."

Liv twisted her head side to side. A moan escaped between her parted lips. When Amber touched her shoulder, Liv lifted her free arm and swung, her fist narrowly missing Amber's jaw.

Finally, Liv's eyes snapped open. Instead of sanity and recognition, they held wildness.

Amber tried again. "It was a dream. You're here with me."

Liv bolted upright and scooted to the far side of the bed. Some of the madness had left her eyes. They were now wide pools of fear. Her chest rose and fell with jagged breaths.

Amber sat on the edge of the bed. "What did you dream?" As soon as the question left her mouth, she had second thoughts. Would talking about it only make things worse?

Liv drew her knees up to her chest and wrapped her arms around her legs. "I dreamed about Landon. It was awful." She drew in a shaky breath. "I saw him in the distance, standing with his back to me. I walked toward him. When I finally got close, he turned around."

Liv shuddered and squeezed her eyes shut. "His face was rotting off and I could see his skull on one side. He reached for me and his fingers brushed my cheek. Flesh was hanging from his hand and arm."

She shuddered again and Amber resisted the urge to shake her head. Liv had seen one too many zombie movies. Amber patted her arm. "It was just a nightmare."

Liv's eyes met hers. "I dream about him a lot. They're not all bad." Her lips curved up in a soft smile. "In some, I find out it was a big misunderstanding, that he didn't really die. But a lot of times, the dreams are like the one tonight."

The smile faded and creases formed between her eyebrows. Her gaze settled on the opposite wall and several seconds passed in contemplative silence. "I know they were taking up for me, but I didn't ask them to."

Uneasiness chewed at the edges of Amber's mind and the temperature seemed to drop several degrees. "What do you mean?"

Liv's gaze snapped back to Amber, realization flooding her eyes. "I mean…I was referring to when we were all there talking and they were sticking up for me." She forced an uneasy laugh. "That didn't come out the way I intended it to."

The uneasiness traveled lower to settle in Amber's gut, which was turning into a solid block of ice. "Vince, Alex and Ray followed through with their threats to make Landon pay, didn't they?"

Her friends had killed Landon. All this time she'd proclaimed their innocence and they were guilty of murder. She closed her eyes, fighting against the nausea rising up inside her. When she looked at Liv again, Liv was chewing her lower lip.

"Tell me what happened." Amber's tone was low but commanding. "I want to know everything."

Liv scooted to the edge of the bed and let her feet rest on the carpet. For several moments she sat rocking back and forth, wringing her hands.

Finally she heaved a sigh. "After I dropped you off, I went home. But the other four stayed. When Landon arrived, the guys beat him bad."

She crossed her arms over her stomach and leaned forward, as if in pain. Amber clenched her jaw. Maybe she should feel sympathy toward Liv, but she didn't. "When did you find this out?"

"The next day. Raymond told me. He was pretty freaked out."

"You knew they'd killed Landon and you lied for them."

"No, they didn't kill him. Landon got away. They chased him, but as drunk as they were, they lost him. A few minutes later they found him lying on the ground. He'd fallen and smashed his head on a rock."

Amber frowned. Liv was lying. Or maybe the others had lied to her. "That doesn't agree with what the medical examiner found." Caleb had given her the details.

"What do you mean?"

"Someone smashed his head in with a rock. If he'd tripped and fallen, he'd have thrown his hands out to try to catch himself. He'd have fallen forward and there would've been dirt on his palms and knees."

"He couldn't catch himself. The guys had tied his hands behind his back with Mona's silk scarf."

Amber let Liv's words sink in. If Landon had been running with his hands tied and stumbled, he could have twisted sideways to keep from falling on his face. The silk wouldn't have left any abrasions, like a rope or wire ties. Except…

"The investigators never found a scarf."

"Mona took it. They didn't want to leave anything that could tie them to Landon's death."

She nodded. "When did you learn all this?"

"The next night. I wish they hadn't told me." Liv put her face in her hands. When she lifted her head, tears streaked her cheeks. "I wasn't there. I never saw his body. But the image of him lying in the woods with his head smashed in has haunted me for the past ten years."

Liv retrieved her purse from the nightstand and pulled out a chocolate bar. "Want some?"

Amber raised her brows. *Really?* Maybe Liv needed comfort food. "No, thanks."

"It's dark chocolate, eighty-five percent. Healthy."

Amber shook her head. The last thing she felt like doing was eating, comfort food or otherwise. "Why didn't anyone tell me?"

Liv broke off a square and took a bite. "The guys thought the fewer people who knew the better."

"Then why did they tell you?" Even then Liv had been ditsy, not the best person to keep such a weighty secret.

"They thought I'd be happy about it, because of the rape. I wasn't." She returned to wringing her hands. "If I'd been there, I would've stopped them. If you hadn't gotten sick, we would have both been there to stop them."

Or if she'd texted Landon and told him not to come, there would have been nothing to stop. A double dose of guilt pressed down on her.

She stood and retrieved her pistol from the dresser. At the open door she turned. "There are a lot of things I wish I could undo."

She stepped into the hall and pulled the

door shut, leaving Liv alone with her chocolate. Sleep was likely to be a long time coming, for both of them. Before Amber even tried, she had a call to make.

She picked up her phone and crawled into bed. Tippy joined her, having ventured from wherever she'd hidden during Liv's nightmare. For several minutes Amber stroked the cat's back, letting her soothing presence still her churning thoughts.

Landon's death had been an accident. There was no brutal killer running around unpunished. His family and friends could finally find closure.

Would it make a difference to the killer? Maybe. Maybe not. But she and Liv weren't involved. That had to count for something.

She brought up her contacts and touched the phone icon next to Caleb's name. There weren't many people she could call at 3:00 a.m. But Caleb would be in the middle of his shift.

She waited through two rings. She'd give him this newest information. Levy County and the FBI would decide what to do with it.

If they could make the information public, maybe it would reach the ears of the killer. Maybe he'd decide justice had been served with the deaths of the four involved and no one else needed to die.

And maybe they'd eventually learn his identity and bring *him* to justice.

Caleb stepped onto Amber's porch and cast a glance over his shoulder. The sun was still so low in the sky the house's shadow stretched all the way to the road. But the heat and humidity already gave hints the day was going to be another scorcher.

He scanned the area, as he'd done before getting out of his truck. A car sat parked in front of the wooded area catty-corner from Amber's house, a deputy inside. Two more deputies would be nearby, much less obvious, patrolling on foot. Other than that, the area appeared deserted.

Caleb reached for the doorbell. Amber's middle-of-the-night call had come out of the blue. But he couldn't say the information had surprised him. It had only confirmed what he'd known all along—Liv and her friends had kept secrets.

Maybe Amber asking Liv to move in with her hadn't been a bad idea. It had only been two days and it was already loosening her tongue.

The door swung inward and Amber invited him inside. She was dressed in jean shorts and a pink T-shirt, her hair drawn up into a high ponytail. Tippy smacked happily at her food dish. Although Amber had apparently been up for a while, Liv was nowhere to be seen.

Fine. He wasn't leaving until he'd questioned her. Her friends weren't as innocent as they'd claimed all these years. And someone knew it. If he could get Liv focused long enough to figure out who, maybe they could solve this thing.

Amber closed the door behind him and motioned toward the couch. "Have a seat. I haven't heard a peep out of Liv, but I'll go ahead and get her up."

She headed toward the hall, her ponytail swinging from side to side. A few seconds later her voice drifted to him. So did Liv's moan. After several sharp raps on the door and more moans of protest, Amber returned to the living room.

"I told her you're here and need to talk to her. She assured me she's getting up."

Nearby, a dresser drawer closed a little harder than necessary, confirmation that although Liv was up, she wasn't happy about it.

Amber sat on the other end of the couch. "Liv's a late sleeper. When I left for work yesterday at almost noon, she still wasn't up." She lowered her voice. "She says it's because of the medication she takes."

"What kind of medication?"

"Antidepressants, I think. And some kind

of antianxiety medication." Her voice dipped even further. "Liv has issues. I knew she wasn't working, but I thought she was between jobs. We talked about it more Sunday night. She's on disability."

Amber sighed. "She's had problems with depression going all the way back to high school. She always acted happy and ditsy, but I knew it was an act. Her home life was miserable. When this happened with Landon, she took it hard. She's let it eat at her for the past ten years."

Caleb nodded and Amber continued.

"Her mental state has really deteriorated since the reunion. Seeing her friends being knocked off one by one, knowing she could be next—she's having a hard time coping with it."

Down the hall, a door creaked open. Liv stumbled into the room looking nowhere near ready to face the day. After rubbing both hands down her face, she squinted at him though half-closed eyes. Her face was clear of the heavy makeup she usually wore and yesterday's gel had left her hair flat in some spots and spiking outward at weird angles in others.

Amber offered her a smile. "Good morning, Liv." Her tone was cheery but her eyes held compassion.

His heart swelled with respect. He wouldn't want to be in her shoes, but if anyone had the patience and empathy to deal with an emotionally fragile roommate, it was Amber.

Liv flopped onto the love seat then repositioned herself to curl her legs under her. "You wanted to talk to me?"

Caleb nodded. "Amber called last night and told me what you'd told her. I'd like to hear it from you."

Liv's gaze shifted to the side and as she spoke, her expression alternated between distant, sad, tortured and blank. When she finished, her eyes again met his. The story she'd related was the same one she'd given Amber.

He crossed one ankle over the other knee and entwined his fingers in his lap. "You said when they found Landon, he was dead. How did they determine that?"

"Alex felt his wrist for a pulse. When he couldn't find one, Vincent rolled him over and felt his neck. He wasn't breathing, either."

"Where was the rock the guys thought he hit his head on?"

"When they got there, he was lying on it. According to Mona, there were several of them around. She said it looked like someone had gathered them. A few were stacked in a small mound and a few more were scattered around. When Raymond realized Landon was dead, he freaked out. He started kicking the rocks and screaming about how they were all going to jail."

"Did you ever see this scarf of Mona's?"

"She was wearing it that night. I guess it was the same one. I never saw her wear it after that."

"You said Raymond is the one who first told you what had happened. Did you ever discuss it with anyone other than Raymond and Mona?"

"Over the next couple of weeks I discussed it with all of them." She cast a glance at Amber. "Except her."

"Did you tell anybody outside your little group?"

"No."

"Did any of the others?"

"Not that I know of."

Amber shifted on the couch next to him. "They wouldn't have needed to. Logan spread the rumor all over town that I coerced Landon to come out to the woods and we killed him."

Amber was right. When investigators had spoken to Logan ten years ago, he'd been quite vocal with his allegations.

"Did you guys ever return to your hangout?"

"Uh-uh. We decided since there was supposedly a killer loose, it might look suspicious if we didn't seem concerned about it. I didn't want to, anyway. Knowing what the others did to Landon, I didn't want to hang out with them anymore."

"Can you think of anything else that might help us figure out who's doing this?"

She shook her head. Apparently Liv had told him everything she knew. The problem was, the people he needed to talk to were dead. Only Vincent, Raymond, Alex and Ramona knew exactly what had happened.

Caleb glanced at his watch. After leaving Amber's, he'd call in the other details he'd received from Liv. Someone would give the new information to the medical examiner and have them take another look at the case to determine whether Landon's death could have happened the way Liv said it had.

But first he'd enjoy a leisurely breakfast with Amber. When he'd told her he was stopping by home to take care of Kira and Tess then heading over, she'd offered to feed him. He never turned down a free meal, especially when it meant not eating alone. Sharing it with Amber was an added plus, even though it would be a threesome.

He looked at Liv. "One more thing. We might see about getting some help from the media."

Liv snapped suddenly to attention. "The media? What do you mean?"

"If we make these new details public, maybe

the killer will hear and realize Landon's death was an accident and you and Amber weren't involved. Maybe a 'What Really Happened to Landon Cleary?' feature."

"No, that's not a good idea." Liv's eyes filled with something bordering on panic.

"We don't have to mention your name."

She straightened her legs and planted both feet on the floor, her posture stiff. "Landon is gone. It's not right to ruin his good name."

Amber spread her arms, palms up. "His good name? After what he did to you, do you really feel he deserves a good name?"

Liv's gaze dipped to her hands, now clutched in her lap. "He's dead. Let him rest in peace."

Amber shook her head. Caleb had the same sentiment. He'd heard of rare instances of rape victims falling in love with their rapists, but he'd never witnessed it firsthand.

"I can't make any promises. The final decision is in the hands of someone whose pay grade is way above mine."

When Amber stood, he pushed himself to his feet to follow her, ready to help with breakfast. He had little interest in cooking alone, but he knew his way around a kitchen. He used to help his wife regularly.

Amber pulled a large bowl from one of the lower cabinets and placed it on the counter, then took a whisk from a drawer. Last, she removed a carton of eggs from the fridge. "You can crack six of these, add a little milk and whip them together."

"I think I can handle it."

The smile she gave him made his insides draw together. As she moved about the room, laying out ingredients for their breakfast casserole, the tightness became an ache.

The things he'd missed over the past four years were too many to count. But it was remembering the insignificant activities that tortured him the most—working in the kitchen together, critiquing movies, talking about current events and crazy fads and sometimes total nonsense.

He pulled his thoughts from things domestic and redirected them toward the case. The killer wasn't likely to strike anytime soon. With Liv and Amber being guarded as closely as heads of state, anyone meaning them harm would be hard pressed to get near them.

Meanwhile, law enforcement would keep working to identify the killer. Maybe someone Logan had talked to had gone overboard and taken it upon himself to mete out justice. Logan probably wasn't experiencing any sorrow over the four who'd been killed. But as the primary suspect, cooperating would be to his advantage.

For Liv's sake, sometime soon, they needed a break. Ever since the reunion, her emotional state had been heading downhill faster than a runaway freight train.

If they didn't solve this case soon, her tenuous grip on sanity was going to disappear altogether.

TEN

Amber forced her eyes open. They immediately drifted closed again. Somewhere in the distance an alarm was going off, a high-pitched squeal.

She tried to ignore it but, if anything, it grew louder, more persistent. Couldn't someone make it stop? She was so tired. All she wanted was to sleep.

Something else was disturbing her peace, too, a plaintive cry, even closer than the alarm. There it was again. And again, more and more frequent. The cry was worse than the alarm. Was it a baby?

Now there were shouts, deep male voices. She dragged her eyes open again and something pungent filled her nostrils.

Smoke.

She bolted upright in bed and tried to shake the sleep from her brain. But her head felt as if it was stuffed full of quilt batting. What was wrong with her?

More shouts sounded from the front yard, followed by the sharp crack of splitting wood. Someone had kicked in the front door.

Now the sources of the other sounds registered. The squeal wasn't an alarm. It was sirens from emergency vehicles. As she sat trying to make sense of everything, they grew louder. Another cry came from under her bed. Tippy.

Her door burst open and she reached for her bedside lamp. Light flooded the room. One of the deputies who'd been guarding her made it to her in two large strides.

She looked around, confusion refusing to release its grip on her befuddled brain. One siren grew to ear-piercing levels then fell silent. A second was still building in volume as it drew closer. A gray haze hung in the air, an even thicker cloud of smoke billowing in through the open door. Her eyes stung and her throat closed in reflex.

Something was on fire.

The deputy grasped her hand. "Come on. We've got to get you out of here."

After he helped her to her feet, a fit of coughing overtook her. She straightened, swiping at the tears streaming down her face. There was something important she was forgetting.

Liv! As heavily as she slept, she'd never wake up on her own.

Before she could say as much, a fur-covered streak shot out from under the bed and into the hall.

"Tippy, no!" Her shout was more of a rasp.

She dashed off after the cat, pointing at the closed spare bedroom door. "Wake Liv up." She clamped a hand over her mouth, determined not to breathe in any more smoke than necessary. But when she got to the end of the hall, she almost gasped. Flames engulfed the kitchen and dining area and were spreading to the living room. As she watched, they climbed over the love seat and danced across its surface.

Tippy apparently had the same stunned reaction. She froze in the center of the room, back arched and tail twice its normal size. After doing a complete one-eighty, seemingly in midair, she darted up the hall and disappeared into the bedroom.

Amber tore off after her. When she passed Liv's room, the door was open and the deputy was rousing Liv. Amber slammed her own door and sucked in a gulp of smoke-filled air, which induced another coughing fit. After recovering, she dropped to her hands and knees. As expected, Tippy had returned to her hiding place under the bed. When Amber reached for her, the cat swatted at her, leaving four bloody streaks down her arm.

She jerked back and stood. How was she going to get Tippy to safety without her escaping? The two cat carriers were in the storage closet off the other end of the kitchen. Even if they were still usable, she'd never be able to reach them.

She glanced around the room then stripped the case from one of her pillows. When she pulled the cat from under the bed, Tippy was all legs and feet, claws extended. More bloody tracks found their way onto her body.

"Tippy, calm down." She plopped the cat onto the bed and gripped her by the scruff of the neck. Tippy flattened her ears and hissed. With her free hand, Amber pulled the pillow case over the squirming body. When that was accomplished, she flipped her upside down and gathered the top edge of the fabric.

"Amber, are you inside?"

The voice belonged to friend and fireman Wade Tanner. She grabbed a fleece robe and threw it over her silk PJs. After slipping her weapon into her purse, she scooped up her squirming bundle and raced into the hall. The smoke had thickened and the entire living room looked to be in flames.

She pulled her robe over her nose. "We're fine. Work on the fire."

As she closed her door the deputy ushered her inside the other bedroom. Liv was standing outside the open window, eyes wide. Amber had never seen her so perky after having just woken up. Apparently Liv needed a life-or-death emergency to get herself moving.

The deputy motioned toward the window. "Now it's your turn."

After she handed the pillow case and her purse to Liv, the deputy knelt, offering her one bent leg to use as a step.

By the time she was on her feet outside, Wade and his partner Joe Stearn had unrolled the fire hose.

Joe walked to the truck, leaving Wade holding the end. The hose swelled and an arc-shaped spray burst from its metal tip.

Amber turned toward the deputy, who had climbed outside. "What happened? Did you see anything?"

"We didn't. By the time we knew something was wrong, the house was already on fire. With the blinds drawn, it was hard to tell what was going on. We saw light inside and realized it didn't look right. Once we figured it out, I called it in then busted the door down to get you ladies out while the other guys went in search of whoever started it."

After taking her items from Liv, she held the pillow case to her chest, cooing softly. Tippy was no longer struggling. Maybe she felt secure in her makeshift cocoon.

As she watched Wade and Joe busy at work, a crushing weight bore down on her, sadness mixed with bone-weary exhaustion. Driven out of her home. Her belongings destroyed. She couldn't think about it tonight. She'd deal with it in the light of a new day.

She leaned against the oak in her front yard and closed her eyes. A wave of dizziness hit her. For the past four nights she'd stayed up far too late talking with Liv. Two of those four nights, she'd had her sleep interrupted.

As far as her fuzzy brain went, all the smoke she'd inhaled likely accounted for part of her problem. Her head hurt and it was still hard to focus. There was no telling what kinds of chemicals were emitted when household items burned.

Soon the fire was out and Wade and Joe rolled up the hose and put their equipment away. Chief Sandlin of the Cedar Key Police Department had arrived, too, and spoken with the deputies. They'd searched the surrounding area and found nothing suspicious. But while checking the house, one of them had discovered the back door unlocked, with a broken pane of glass near the doorknob. Since they patrolled constantly, leaving no section of the house out of sight for more than a minute or so, they couldn't explain how someone was able to get in, set the fire and get out without being seen.

Wade approached. "Are you sure you don't need any kind of medical treatment?"

Liv shook her head and Amber did, too. Once the chemicals dissipated, she'd feel fine. If not, she'd go to the doctor.

Wade continued. "This will be investigated as arson, so you're not going to be able to go inside for a few days. Once the investigators clear it, we'll let you know."

Amber looked at the house with its splintered door jamb and burned-out interior. First thing in the morning, she'd call her landlord, who spent summers in New York.

As far as her possessions, she had them insured. Most of what she'd lost could be replaced. What couldn't...well, she and Liv had made it out, and she had her cat. Her and Liv's and Tippy's safety was all that mattered.

If she still had all five cats, she'd never have gotten them all out. Caleb had pushed her to return the four foster cats. She owed him a huge thank-you.

As if her thoughts had conjured him up, a blue Ford F-150 screeched to a stop across the street and Caleb jumped out. He raced toward her through the beams of the fire truck's headlights. As he drew closer, his gaze swept her from head to toe.

He grasped her by the shoulders and his mouth met hers in a sudden, emotional kiss. It was fast, a little rough and impulsive, but she felt it all the way to her toes.

Before she could recover, he wrapped his arms around her, his face pressed into her hair. "I heard your house was on fire and you were inside. I was so worried."

Between them, Tippy squirmed and emitted a muffled meow.

He stepped away but instead of releasing her, he held her at arm's length. For several moments he stared, as if trying to convince himself that she was all right.

She answered his unspoken question. "We're fine. The fire started in the kitchen. We were in our bedrooms with the doors closed. Tippy woke me up meowing."

He dropped his hands and smiled. "Watch cat."

"Actually, it was the combination of Tippy

meowing, the sirens squealing and the deputy hollering. I was sleeping like a log." She sighed. "I guess I'm going back to my brother's house. Liv will have to sleep on the couch. I might take you up on your offer to keep Tippy."

"I think you'll be able to take her with you."

She looked up at him, brows raised, and he continued.

"My aunt and uncle had a small horse farm this side of Ocala. It's for sale, but I discussed it with them as a possible place for you to hide out if the need arose. I've run it by everyone involved in the case, too, and they agreed it would make a great safe house."

Liv nodded, her eyes bright. "It sounds perfect."

Amber released a frustrated sigh. That was easy for Liv to say. She didn't have responsibilities.

"I can't leave. I have a full-time job."

Even as she made her objections, her pulse fluttered. Maybe the kiss was nothing more than an expression of overwhelming relief. But the fact that Caleb would go to this much trouble to see to her safety had to mean something.

She cast a sideways glance at the house she'd called home for the past year, half of which was now a burned-out shell. That was what could happen to people who associated with her.

"I can't put your family at risk."

Caleb again gripped her shoulders. "I told them about you. They want to help. Over the years, at least a dozen troubled kids have come through their doors. That's the kind of people they are."

He slid his hands down her arms to take her hands. "This will be much safer. Instead of being surrounded by trees, their place sits in the middle of acres of pastureland. There are woods nearby, but nothing within a hundred feet. No one will get anywhere near you or Liv without us seeing him."

"What about my job?" She offered one last protest, but her objections were losing their strength.

"I'm sure Chief Sandlin will hold your position until this is over. If there's any doubt, I can go ask him right now." He tilted his head toward the other end of the house, where her chief stood talking to one of the deputies.

She nodded slowly, letting Caleb's words sink in. What he said made sense. The killer had a way of slipping in and out undetected, right under the noses of law enforcement. She'd never seen anything like it. But this would make it much harder for him.

"All right. We'll do it."

The last thing she wanted was to put someone else's possessions at risk.

But maybe it was the only way.

Caleb turned onto 225 and stepped on the gas. This was horse country. Mile after mile of fence stretched along each side of the road, bordering pastures, green, almost flat and seemingly unending. A sign marked the drive to each farm. His uncle's place would be a couple miles up on the left. At one time, a sign had read Lyons Quarter Horses. It was now gone.

A mix of nostalgia and sadness rolled though him. He'd always loved the farm and had made a lot of good memories there.

When he'd learned two years ago that his aunt and uncle had begun to sell off the horses, he'd known the day was coming when they'd no longer be able to keep things up. Actually he'd known it before that. They'd been slowing down for the past five years.

Six months ago they'd left the farmhouse to move into a double-wide mobile home on a postage-stamp-size lot in one of those senior communities. The old house had sat empty ever since. Until now.

He moved his foot to the brake and checked his rearview mirror. When he'd made the trip yesterday, Amber had followed him in her

RAV4, Liv and a couple of deputies behind her. They'd had a regular convoy going. Today, no one followed him. Unfortunately.

With law enforcement personnel along the road and in the woods and one stationed inside at all times, the killer would find himself walking into a trap. It was exactly what Caleb wanted.

He made a sharp left and his turn signal clicked off. The long, dirt drive stretched ahead of him, the old farmhouse at its end. It needed a coat of paint and the rocking chairs that had lent a sort of coziness had long been removed, but the charm of the place was still there.

Three dormer windows jutted out from the second story, the one on the left marking the room he'd slept in during spring and summer breaks. A porch wrapped all four sides, inviting visitors to relax and enjoy the tranquility of the surroundings.

He drew to a stop at the end of the drive. It wouldn't be dark for another hour, but the lights inside the house were on. A soft glow leaked out from the edges of the drawn curtains.

He stepped from the truck and glanced around him. Except for the occasional scrub oak, the pastures were devoid of trees, leaving almost nowhere for someone to hide. The woods at the perimeter of the property were too far away to hold any real threats.

Before heading to the house, he circled the truck to retrieve a laptop case and two plastic bags from the passenger seat. Yesterday they'd stopped in Williston to pick up some necessities. This morning Amber had requested some more items. No, *requested* was a little tame. *Begged* was more like it.

He stepped onto the porch and moved toward the double front doors. They were set back several feet, forming a protected alcove between the living room on one side and the family room on the other. Since he'd left yesterday, someone had brought the wicker love seat out and positioned it diagonally, still leaving a clear entry path on the right-hand side.

Instead of shifting the items he held, Caleb tapped on the door with one sneakered foot, his lips curving into a smile. Poor Amber. She'd likely not been this idle since...ever. Although his aunt and uncle had at one time had both internet and cable, now there was neither. Cell service was even sketchy. And Amber was climbing the walls from boredom. Though that was probably just part of her problem. Being locked up with Liv 24/7 would be enough to drive anyone to the brink of insanity.

The library books he'd picked up should help pass the time. He also had a surprise for her— his spare laptop and several DVDs from his own collection. Hopefully she liked action adventure. Chick flick options were a little sparse at his place.

The door swung inward. Instead of Amber or Liv, one of the deputies stood there. Caleb breathed a sigh of relief. He'd installed a peephole yesterday, but until this was over, Amber and Liv didn't need to be answering doors.

The deputy invited him in, then closed and locked the door behind him. A smooth voice spilled into the foyer from the room on the left, a female meteorologist giving the weather report.

Caleb held up the two bags. "Emergency supplies for the ladies."

When Amber stepped into the foyer, the smile she gave him lit her eyes. His thoughts drifted to the same place he'd been trying to avoid since early yesterday morning.

He'd kissed her. It had been on impulse. He wasn't even an impulsive kind of guy. What had he been thinking?

Actually he hadn't been. He'd been so relieved to see her standing there unharmed, his brain had apparently shut down.

And he'd hardly thought of anything else since.

Her gaze dipped to what he held and her smile widened. "Is that what I think it is?"

"If you're thinking an attempted cure to your boredom, the answer is yes."

"You're awesome." She took the bag of books from him and eyed the other bags. "Can you hang out awhile?"

"Till a little after ten."

"Good. Let's have a seat. I want to check out my goodies. It feels like Christmas in July."

He followed her to the living room, where Liv was watching the evening news.

Or maybe Amber had been the one watching it. Liv was lying curled up on the couch, face toward the back. Her tank top had hiked up, leaving a couple of inches of skin exposed over the waistband of her shorts.

Greenish-blue ink marked the space, the hearts now top and bottom. Viewed sideways, the swirl circling her initials looked more like a treble clef than a random design.

Caleb laid the laptop bag on the coffee table, took a seat and tilted his head toward the sleeping figure on the opposite couch. "Is she musical?" All his years in band, he'd never seen her.

"I don't think so. Why?"

"Her tattoo. The design wrapping her initials is a sideways treble clef."

"She doesn't play an instrument or sing. She says she can't carry a tune in a bucket." After plopping the bag of books on the coffee table, Amber sat next to him and reached for the second plastic bag. "More goodies?"

Liv stirred. "Can y'all keep it down?"

Amber rolled her eyes and rose. Still holding the last bag he'd given her, she grabbed up the other one from the table and walked from the room. He followed with the laptop bag.

In the foyer, she leaned toward him, her voice a whisper. "That woman has the strangest sleep schedule of anyone I know. She wants to stay up talking half the night, then takes naps at weird times throughout the day."

She blew out a breath that ruffled her bangs. But even her exasperation seemed good-natured. It took a lot for Amber to lose patience.

When she transferred both bags to the same hand and moved toward the front door, he frowned. "Where do you think you're going?"

"The front porch. Who do you think dragged the love seat out there after you left yesterday?"

After standing on tiptoe to look through the peephole, she turned to face him. "If I stay cooped up inside with the curtains drawn, I really will go crazy." She cast a glance at the deputy. "Looks like it's all clear."

The deputy opened the door a crack, his body

blocking the opening, then swung it wider and stepped away.

Caleb pursed his lips. Apparently this was something they'd worked out in his absence. And he didn't like it one bit.

"You're supposed to stay inside." His tone was stern.

Amber stepped outside and sat on the love seat. "Look." She set both bags at her feet to indicate the view with a wave of her hand. "What do you see?"

He followed her gaze. The dirt driveway seemed to go on forever, clumps of grass separating two parallel tracks. From his vantage point, an angled portion of each side of the front yard was visible, the angle narrowing as it reached the house. Across the street, horses grazed in another pasture. Beyond that, the sun rested on the tops of distant trees, staining the sky shades of orange, pink and lavender.

Amber continued her defense. "We're protected. Someone would have to be in the driveway to even know we're here. And by the time they made it to the house, we could be in the next county. And don't forget about the law enforcement personnel everywhere."

He heaved a reluctant sigh. He had to cut her some slack. He couldn't handle being cooped up with Liv without some means of escape, either.

"Now, to check out these goodies." She leaned forward to pull the books from the bag then placed them in her lap. "Seven. One a day for the next week." She thumbed through them. "A romance. Another romance. And…another romance."

When she smiled over at him, his chest tightened. *Oh, no.* Hopefully she wouldn't read anything into what he'd picked.

"I figured all women like to read romance novels. But I got help. The librarian chose these."

Amber checked out the last four. "Young adult. Another young adult. Fantasy. And this one looks like women's fiction."

"One missing genre is suspense. I didn't think you'd appreciate a woman-in-jeopardy story."

When she looked at him again, appreciation shone from her eyes. "You're awesome."

She'd called him that twice in the span of five minutes. Coming from Amber, it had a pleasant ring. "You're easy to please."

"I am, but that's beside the point." She returned the books to the bag and set the other one in her lap. "DVDs." Her excitement dimmed. "There's nothing to play them on. I already looked."

"There is now." He unzipped the black bag and removed the laptop. "This one's a spare. You can use it as long as you'd like."

She twisted in the seat to throw both arms around his neck. "You're the best."

He returned her hug, ending with two casual pats on her back. He'd been worried about her reading something into his choice of novels, when it was his own thoughts he needed to corral.

She released him to pick up the first movie and read the blurb. "This looks exciting."

He crossed an ankle over one knee, his right arm resting on the wicker arm of the chair and his left draped across the back, behind Amber. After looking at each of the DVDs, she held up a CD. It had a homemade label with a June 18 date, the words "Peter's Restoration" and the name and address of his church.

"What is this one? Actually, it doesn't matter. I'm about bored enough to listen to people count sheep. In Arabic."

He laughed. "It's a sermon tape from about three weeks ago. I thought you might enjoy it. My pastor's good."

"A sermon tape?" She gave him a crooked smile. "You think God is the answer for everything that ails us."

"I do."

She returned the CD to the bag with the other items. "Sometimes life's a little more complicated than that."

"It's a lot *less* complicated when you're not trying to do everything on your own."

For a good half minute she kept her eyes downcast as she fiddled with the handle of the plastic bag. Finally her gaze traveled down the drive then lifted to settle on the sky far in the distance. During the short time they'd sat, the colors had deepened, a testament to the power and creativity of God.

She sighed. "I don't even know how to get there."

"The road back can seem long and winding, but He's never more than a prayer away."

She gave him a rueful smile. "Easy for you to say. You've never had to find your way back. You've always lived a perfect life."

"I'm not perfect. Not by a long shot."

It wasn't the first time she'd made that accusation. Maybe it was time to dispel the false notion once and for all.

He moved his arm from behind her to clasp his hands in his lap. "I told you about my wife being killed. What I didn't tell you was how I handled it."

Several seconds of silence passed before Amber spoke. "Before now, I would have guessed you had some powerful testimony about how you leaned on God and He carried you through the darkest time of your life. But that's not the story you're about to tell me, is it?"

"Not at all." He drew in a deep breath. "We were living in Orlando at the time. I left my church there, sold our house, quit the Orlando Police Department and returned to Chiefland. That's when I went to work for Levy County. It took me a whole year, though, to find my way back into church. I was angry with God. I felt I'd been doing everything right and He took away the only thing in my life that mattered."

He shook his head. "A friend of mine went through something similar a couple of years later. He was a rock. He was completely broken, but he clung to his faith like a drowning man holding on to a life raft. And God saw him through."

He took in a slow, deep breath and released it in a heavy sigh. "You know what I did? I cursed God. Then I didn't speak to Him for almost a year. I thought I had a strong faith, but it had never been tested. When it finally was, I failed miserably."

He closed his eyes. God had forgiven him. But it still bothered him. And he'd never found the confidence that, if it happened again, he'd handle it any better than he had the first time.

A soft hand slid between his clasped ones and fingers entwined with his. He opened his eyes to see Amber looking up at him, her gaze filled with sympathy and understanding.

"Thank you for sharing with me. For being real. That's what those of us on the outside need to see." She turned her head and focused on a point in the distance. Her face took on an expression of contemplation. "It gives us hope." Her last words were barely audible.

Was the shell around her heart starting to crack? One thing he knew for sure, sitting here next to her, his fingers entwined with hers, somehow felt right. Over the past few weeks she'd woven right past every defense he possessed and found her way into his heart.

At first she'd just intrigued him. Soon that interest had turned to respect and admiration. She was as beautiful on the inside as she was on the outside. She had a giving spirit. She was kind and compassionate. There wasn't a selfish bone in her body. She exuded sweetness and even had a good sense of humor.

She had all the qualities he wanted in a woman.

There was only one problem. He'd already

laid it all out with God. He was willing to consider another romantic relationship.

But no cops.

Unfortunately, God didn't seem to be listening.

ELEVEN

Credits rolled on the screen and music blared, tense and driving. Actually the whole movie had been tense, almost nonstop excitement. It had been well worth ninety minutes of her time, even watching it on a laptop screen. The only things missing were her cats. She had Tippy, but ever since they'd arrived, the cat had holed up in the bedroom and refused to come out. Amber had finally given up and relocated both the litter box and the food and water dishes.

After swinging her feet from the coffee table to the floor, she leaned forward to turn off the DVD. The sudden silence was a sharp contrast to the drums, trumpets and electric guitar that had poured from the computer's internal speakers.

She pressed a button on the side of the laptop and a drawer popped open.

"What did you think of the movie?" It was the second of Caleb's they'd watched.

Liv lifted a shoulder in a one-sided shrug. "It was good."

After removing the DVD, Amber popped it into its plastic case and snapped it closed. When she looked at Liv again, she was sitting with her head tilted to the side, her gaze fixed on an invisible spot on the coffee table.

"Everything okay?"

That probably wasn't a good question. Where Liv was concerned, things were *never* okay. Once the killer was found and brought to justice, maybe she could get back to her therapist and find help for her problems.

The other shoulder came up this time. "I was thinking about Landon."

"You seem to do a lot of that."

"Don't you?" She looked off into the distance. "You should."

"Pardon me?"

"I mean, you were dating him, right?"

"No. Remember? He'd asked me out. We hadn't had our first date. Once I found out about what he did to you, there's no way I would've gone out with him."

Liv crossed her arms. "Were you in love with him?" The question sounded almost accusatory.

"No. I was interested in him, like every other girl in the school. But I wasn't in love with him. I was surprised when he asked me out."

Liv nodded slowly, as if trying to make sense of the answer. Or maybe she was reading between the lines, searching for hidden meanings. There weren't any.

For the next several seconds a sort of brooding silence stretched between them. That was typical of Liv. Her emotions bounced all over the spectrum.

Amber stood, ready to go to the kitchen in search of a healthy midafternoon snack.

Before she reached the open doorway, Liv's voice stopped her.

"Landon was a good man. He didn't deserve to die."

Amber did a double-take. "Whatever punishment he deserved is governed by our justice system, but anyone who would rape a woman is not a good man."

"But…"

Amber walked toward Liv then stopped to look down at her from the other side of the coffee table. "But what?"

"I don't remember." Liv picked up the remote and clicked on the TV, indicating the conversation was over.

Fine. She'd just read. Or maybe she'd listen to Caleb's sermon CD. She wasn't likely to hear anything life-changing, but learning she'd listened to it would make Caleb happy.

It beat zoning out in front of the TV. There was no satellite here, not even cable. The flat plate mounted on the wall was one step up from the old-fashioned rabbit ears. It gave them a few choices—if they didn't mind some snow and static.

Amber picked up the laptop and retrieved the CD from the stack of movies on the corner of the coffee table. Caleb would be there in a couple of hours with pizza and salad fixings. Meanwhile, she'd grab some baby carrots and go chill in her room.

A few minutes later she was stretched out on the bed, hands folded over her stomach, eyes closed. The paper towel that had held the carrots was wadded up on the nightstand and Caleb's laptop sat open beside her on the bed.

A commanding bass voice came from the laptop's speaker as Caleb's pastor read. Jesus and his disciples were at the last supper when Jesus predicted one of them would betray him. That would have been Judas. Anyone who'd ever sat through a Palm Sunday or Easter service probably knew the story.

The chapter ended with Peter swearing he was ready to die for Christ. The guy had been a little overconfident. She knew what happened next. While Jesus was being tried, Peter was in the courtyard warming himself by the fire. Three different times, Peter denied even knowing Jesus. That was another part of the Easter story.

Sure enough, the pastor skipped to John 18 to read all the incriminating details. Poor Peter. Failures memorialized for generations to come.

She drew in a breath and let it out in a relaxed sigh. This was turning out to be more interesting than she'd expected, which maybe was nothing more than a testament to how bored she was. But she had to agree with Caleb. His pastor was a good speaker. The deep, smooth voice with lots of inflection and interesting commentary held her attention. This was no dry recitation of scripture.

After reading another passage wherein the resurrected Jesus gave Peter the opportunity to confess his love, the pastor wrapped up his message, summarizing his points.

"No matter how awful your past may be, Jesus is ready to not only forgive you, but also to restore you. But you have to be completely honest about where you are."

Where was she right now? Racked with guilt, still unable to let it go ten years later.

And trying to do enough good to atone for all her past wrongs. Just as Caleb had said. She could no longer deny it.

Last week Hunter's pastor had preached about David, how he'd messed up royally but still found his way back. This afternoon it was Peter.

There was also Caleb's story. Like Peter, maybe he'd been overconfident. Whatever the cause, he'd suffered his own failures.

Sunday, she'd wondered if God was trying to tell her something. Now the answer seemed like a definitive yes.

In the span of seven days, God had given her three life-changing examples. The stories were different, but the basic pattern was the same— failure, forgiveness, restoration. It was exactly what she needed.

Could she do it? Could she let go of the wrong she'd done when the consequences were all around her? Could she find a way back to the faith of her early childhood?

A light clicked on in her brain and she unclasped her hands to push herself to an upright position. Yes she could.

Actually she'd been trying. But she'd gone about it all wrong. Nothing she could do would make her worthy of forgiveness. She could see it now. All the hours she spent doing good, the time was never wasted. But it didn't do anything to get her one step closer to God or to cancel out a single one of her past mistakes.

Only one thing could do that. Forgiveness was being offered freely, because Christ loved her enough to pay the ultimate price.

She swung her legs over the side of the bed, stood then dropped to her knees. In that pose of humility, it finally came together, everything she'd learned in her childhood. She surrendered it all to God—her will, her regrets, her mistakes.

When she rose to her feet, she was a changed person. For the first time in over ten years the burden of guilt was gone, replaced with a sense of peace. She wasn't naive enough to believe life would be perfect from then on. But right now, nothing could dim her joy.

She had to share. What she'd found was exactly what Liv needed.

She hurried from the room and bounded down the stairs. When she entered the living room, Liv was pushing herself to a seated position, her eyes still half closed. Amber had apparently interrupted one of her naps.

Liv wrinkled her nose. "What's wrong with you?"

"Nothing's wrong. In fact, I've never been—" She swallowed the rest of her words as Liv's frown deepened. This wouldn't be the best time to talk to her. She'd be much more receptive when she was in a better mood. But she had to tell someone.

Caleb. No, he'd probably already left his house by now. She wouldn't call him while he was driving.

Her parents. They'd be as happy as Caleb. They'd both sent up a lot of tearful prayers over the past fifteen years.

She headed toward the foyer to go back upstairs, where she wouldn't disturb Liv. Too bad she didn't have anything appropriate to celebrate with. Because that was exactly what she felt like doing. A big party, complete with cake and ice cream. Or chocolate. Dark chocolate.

She cast a glance over her shoulder. "Did you bring any of that chocolate with you?"

Liv opened one eye. She'd already lain down again. "There's a half bar in my purse. It's on my nightstand."

Amber took the steps two at a time. At Liv's closed door, she hesitated. Walking into her room felt like an invasion of her privacy. But if Liv had had a problem with it, she'd have gotten the chocolate herself. Or she'd have said she didn't have any. Liv obviously didn't have any qualms about lying.

Amber opened the door and when she stepped into the room, she let out a low whistle. She was no neat freak, but considering they'd only been there two days, the room was a disaster. Makeup and hair products were spread out across the dresser, and every piece of clothing Liv had brought with her, lay scattered about the room.

Amber picked up Liv's pajamas and laid them on the bed before stepping up to the nightstand. Her purse was there, along with four prescription medicine bottles and a journal. Writing out her thoughts and feelings was probably therapeutic for Liv.

Hopefully she was doing it. Amber cracked the book open to peek inside.

Yes, Liv was using the journal. The page was half filled, six lines, anyway. But this wasn't a typical journal entry. It was a poem.

She opened the book fully. She'd had no intention of snooping through Liv's things, but something unsettling chewed at the edges of her mind. She scanned the words.

The darkness weaves a path right to my heart,
A thick, inky poison that will not part.
It travels higher to capture my mind,
A smothering blanket that leaves me blind.
I'm trapped inside the blackest of night.
Then blood flows—a glimmer of light.

Amber's skin prickled and the fine hairs on the back of her neck stood on end.

A poem. Six lines. Was this left by the killer in a note to Liv and she wrote about it, transferring the poem to her journal? Or had Liv written the poem herself?

Amber picked up the journal and turned the page. It was another poem, same rhyming style as the one before it. And every bit as dark and disturbing. Amber flipped two more pages and read their contents, her mind trying to untangle what this meant while at the same time searching for an alternative to the obvious.

Liv couldn't be the killer. She'd gotten the same threats as the rest of them. Whoever had targeted the others had also targeted Liv. He'd made threatening phone calls. He'd tried to break into her house. He'd even fired shots into her window.

All this according to Liv. Had the reports been fabricated? Was she the one who'd fired the shots? She could have been. No one had witnessed any of the incidents.

Amber plopped the journal onto the bedside stand. She could deny it no longer.

Liv was the killer.

Amber whirled around.

Liv stood in the open doorway, her left

index finger over her mouth in a command to be silent.

Her right hand held a pistol.

Caleb pulled out of the ABC Pizza parking lot, his stomach rumbling. Tantalizing aromas wafted to him from the passenger seat.

He'd ordered two large pizzas with everything on them. They could each have their fill tonight and the ladies would have some leftover for lunch tomorrow.

A traffic light ahead changed and he slowed to a stop, glancing in the rearview mirror. Through the next two turns, he did the same thing, keeping a diligent watch behind him. No one appeared to be following him.

He heaved a sigh. This was his third trip to his aunt and uncle's place. He'd even driven to Amber's house to check out the progress of the investigation. The official report wasn't available yet, but the fire was looking more and more like arson.

Wherever he'd gone, no one had paid him a bit of attention. If the killer didn't make a move soon, they'd have to do something different. His aunt and uncle had agreed to take the house off the market temporarily. But he couldn't expect them to do it forever.

Besides, Amber's patience was going to

eventually run out, if not with Liv, then with the entire situation. She was more than ready to return to her normal life—her job with Cedar Key, her foster cats, her work with the hospice. Being idle was about to drive her crazy. They needed to get this thing solved.

So far, they had four bodies and no suspect. Except Logan, who hadn't had any involvement in the last two murders. At least, not directly.

They needed to think outside the box, beyond the obvious, and turn any preconceived notions upside down. The first assumption they'd made was that the killer was someone they knew.

That was likely correct. They not only knew the killer, but knew him closely enough for at least one of them to have felt comfortable talking. Or maybe Logan had put someone up to it. But why would anyone want to take up someone else's vendetta?

They'd made another assumption on a more subconscious level. They usually referred to the killer in the masculine. But did it have to be a man?

Ramona had been beaten brutally, but even someone slight of frame could do a lot of damage wielding a baseball bat. Alex had fallen from a balcony. He was tall, six foot five. His center of gravity would have been well above the height of the wrought-iron railing. If he'd been leaning over the edge, as inebriated as he was, a weaker person could have pushed him to his death.

Then there was Vincent, lured into the woods and shot. Armed, the suspect wouldn't need size or strength. But how had Vincent gotten into that position in the first place? His car had checked out fine, so he'd apparently stopped willingly, which would support the assumption he'd known and trusted the killer.

Last was Raymond. The killer had taken out the deputy first then gone in pursuit of Raymond, who'd likely panicked and lost control of his car. To take out a cop in a moving vehicle, the killer was obviously an expert shot. Being ex-military, Logan had the skills. But he'd been nowhere in the area at the time of the deputy's murder. As far as Caleb knew, none of his other classmates were expert marksmen, except a couple who'd gone into law enforcement.

And Liv. According to Amber, Liv had been an excellent shot in high school, had done a lot of competing and won ribbons. But she no longer had a gun. Supposedly.

Liv wasn't right, though. Amber had told him she carried a lot of guilt over what happened to Landon, even though she'd had no part in his death. Could the guilt have broken her?

He stifled a snort. Now he was grasping at straws. Liv was one of the victims, not the suspect. Besides, after being raped, she shouldn't hold any kinds of warm feelings toward Landon.

But she obviously did.

The image of an inked design slid into his mind. A treble clef wrapped her initials. According to Amber, Liv didn't play an instrument or sing. But Landon had been in the band all through high school and had signed Amber's yearbook with a treble clef after his name.

Had Liv been in love with Landon Cleary and that was why she'd wrapped her initials in his symbol? Whoever heard of having one's own initials tattooed on one's body, anyway?

Caleb's eyes widened and he gripped the wheel more tightly. Maybe *LC* didn't stand for *Liv Chamberlain*. Maybe it was for *Landon Cleary*. A permanent remembrance of the man she'd loved and lost.

He jammed on the brakes and pulled off the road, then grabbed his phone. As he swiped the screen, his hand shook. Liv was possibly the killer. And Amber was alone with her.

No, she wasn't alone. Along with law enforcement personnel parked down the road and hiding in the woods, one was also in the house. Besides…

He dropped his hand to his lap. Liv had been as closely guarded as Amber, at least during Raymond's murder and the shooting of the deputy watching him. During the Fourth of July, when someone had come out to Amber's uncle's ranch, Liv had been confined in her house, sick with the flu, two deputies outside. She couldn't have been involved in either incident.

He pulled back onto the road and stepped on the gas. There was something he was missing. Something important.

During his years on the force, he'd learned to go with his gut. And right now his gut was telling him something wasn't right. No matter how he tried to rationalize it away, he couldn't deny the sense of uneasiness hanging over him.

A premonition that wouldn't go away.

Amber's mind spun, the persuasive words she needed lost somewhere in the maelstrom of shock, hurt and fear. "Why?"

Liv stepped inside and closed the door. It made the softest click, but there was something terrifying about the sound. Liv leaned against the wooden surface, her feet shoulder-width apart, weapon aimed at Amber's torso.

Amber's was on her hip. But if she attempted to draw it, Liv would put a bullet through her chest before the pistol even left its holster.

"To right a wrong."

Yeah, she'd gathered that from the poems. "That's what the guys were trying to do. They were trying to make Landon pay for what he did to you. But they didn't mean to kill him. You said that yourself."

"It doesn't matter. They were still to blame. But that's not why they had to die."

It isn't? If not for killing Landon, why?

"Eight months ago, I ran into Vincent. When I saw him looking so happy with his pretty wife and fancy car, it did something to me. All these years I'd been tormented, but he'd moved on without giving Landon's death a second thought. I had to see if the rest of you had done the same thing."

As Liv spoke, Amber angled her body slightly away from Liv and moved her right hand toward her hip one slow inch at a time. She might not be able to draw her weapon before Liv decided to shoot, but the closer she could get, the better chance she'd have. Fractions of seconds counted.

"I went to see Mona first." Liv's gaze dipped to Amber's arm. "Keep your hands where I can see them. Better yet, raise them. Reach for the ceiling."

Amber complied. Liv pressed the barrel of

the pistol into Amber's chest and unsnapped the holster.

"You won't be needing this anymore." Without taking her eyes from Amber's face, she withdrew the weapon from its case and walked backward to the dresser. Then she dropped the gun inside a drawer and pushed it closed.

"Okay. You can put your hands down. Now, back to Mona. She'd gotten a promotion at work and was dating a new guy. She invited me to have dinner with them. She was radiant. It was sickening."

Liv wrinkled her nose and lifted her upper lip as if she'd smelled something pungent. "I went back to her house later and asked her to go for a ride with me. When we got to a wooded area, I made her get out of the car. I had my gun, but I decided that was too quick and painless for her and used the baseball bat instead."

An involuntary shudder shook Amber's shoulders. "Why?"

"She let the guys use her scarf to tie Landon's hands. Because of that he couldn't defend himself."

Liv leaned against the dresser. "With Mona gone, I still needed to take care of Vince and locate you, Alex and Ray.

"So you posed as Mona on Facebook and sent each of us messages to come to the reunion."

"It was perfect timing, a way to observe you all at once. And I saw you had completely moved past what you'd done. Not one of you was mourning his passing."

"I guarantee you, it has haunted every one of us. We just hid it well."

"None of you mourned him like you should have. That's why I had to step in, to get justice for Landon."

Amber shook her head, trying to clear her thoughts. Liv was behind everything—the Facebook messages, the poems, the deaths. The fire...

Amber's eyes widened. "You set the fire, didn't you?"

"You were supposed to stay asleep."

Amber dredged up the details of that night, the trouble she'd had waking up, the fogginess she'd blamed on chemicals she'd inhaled. Realization slammed into her. Liv had poured them each a glass of orange juice before bed.

"You drugged my juice."

Liv didn't respond. A heavy silence settled over the room, broken only by the rhythmic ticking of the wind-up alarm clock on the nightstand. Caleb was due to arrive around six for dinner. What was it now? Five fifteen? Five thirty?

She didn't dare turn to check. Liv knew as

well as she did that when Caleb arrived he'd come looking for them. Any reminder might encourage Liv to speed up what she felt she needed to do. Meanwhile, she'd try to keep Liv talking. "How did you get away without anyone seeing you when we had law enforcement guarding us twenty-four-seven?"

She shrugged. "It wasn't that difficult. I have my brother's old pickup. Shortly after starting all this, I made up a temporary tag and moved it into the woods on the vacant lot behind my house. All I had to do was wait until the cop outside walked around the side of the house. Then I slipped out the back door and hid behind the hedge. Once I got to the corner, it was a short jog to the trees. The truck has worked great for transporting my kayak, too."

Liv had a kayak? That explained how she was able to get off the island and hide out while Amber had investigated the two suspicious calls. With all the little islands surrounded by mangroves, disappearing had been easy.

"The Fourth of July—you were out at my uncle's place, weren't you?"

Instead of responding, Liv shifted her gaze to the nightstand. "I saw you looking at my journal. What do you think of my poetry?"

"It's good. I didn't know you wrote poetry."

"It's a more recent hobby. One of my therapists recommended that I start journaling, writing down my feelings. This is much more creative."

Amber nodded slowly. The whole scene seemed surreal. It was like a casual conversation between friends. Except for the gun.

Liv's gaze drifted past her and Amber eyed the door six feet away. If she inched closer, Liv may not notice. But she'd never be able to swing it open unless something distracted Liv.

"I was in love with him, you know." Liv's words cut into her thoughts. "I'd had a crush on him since seventh grade. But I lost my heart to him our senior year. We had algebra together. We spent hours staying after school, working on assignments."

Amber swallowed hard. "I had no idea you had feelings for him. I thought he was just tutoring you."

Liv's gaze snapped to Amber's face and her lips pulled back in a sneer. "Do you really think I needed all that help? I'm not stupid, you know. It was an excuse to be able to spend time with him." She drew in a deep breath and let it out in a long sigh. "Three weeks before graduation, I finally got up the nerve to tell him how I felt. You know what he did?"

Liv's voice was raised, but with the door closed and the room being at the far end of the hall, it wouldn't carry all the way down to the deputy.

"He snubbed me. And I know why." Both her tone and her eyes were filled with accusation. "It was because he had his eye on you. You ruined everything."

Amber's jaw dropped. "He raped you."

Liv continued as if she hadn't spoken. "We could've had something special if you hadn't gotten in the way."

"How can you say that? Are you forgetting he raped you?"

"No."

The single word was soft but somehow heavy with meaning. A seed of doubt sprouted in Amber's chest, the sense that Liv had kept something important from her.

"No, what?" That she hadn't forgotten? Or was no the answer to an entirely different question, one she didn't know to ask?

"Landon never raped me."

Amber stepped backward, the air whooshing out of her lungs. She'd just taken a steel-toed boot to the gut. A rape that had never taken place had caused an innocent young man's death. Her jaw dropped open but no sound came out.

Liv's eyes dipped to the hardwood floor. "I couldn't stand the thought of seeing you two together. So I made up the story about the rape, knowing you wouldn't go out with him if you believed he'd raped me."

Amber leaned against the nightstand, her legs feeling as if the bones had dissolved. "I wouldn't have gone out with him if you'd told me you had feelings for him."

"I didn't think it through. That was my spur-of-the-moment response. I had no idea the guys would react the way they did. I tried to stop them."

When Liv's eyes again met Amber's, tears had gathered on her lower lashes. "The guys and Mona have paid for their sins. Now it's just you and me."

Liv raised her left arm to take a two-handed grip.

Amber's pulse shot to double time and panic pounded up her spine. "You think I haven't grieved over what happened to Landon, but I have. As much as you have. For the last ten years I've run like a crazy person, trying to stay a step ahead of the guilt and regret always dogging me. I finally found relief this afternoon. You can, too."

Amber held out a hand and moved slowly forward. Somewhere in the distance, a step creaked. Was the deputy coming up the stairs?

Had something tipped him off? Or was she hearing the old house settle?

Another creak sounded. Someone was definitely approaching. And trying to be stealthy. She had to distract Liv.

She took another step forward, arm extended. "Lower the gun. We'll get you some help. It doesn't have to be like this." She took another step.

"Stop!" The word was like the crack of a whip.

Amber froze and Liv continued. "You've been so nice to me. I don't want you to suffer."

"Then don't do this."

"It was your text that got Landon out there, so you need to pay. But I'll make it sure and quick, a bullet straight through the heart."

"If you shoot me, the cop downstairs will be in here in about ten seconds flat."

"And he'll find us both dead. After I kill you, the next bullet is for me."

There was another footfall in the hall and another, both almost soundless. Whoever was there would be close enough now to hear their conversation. *God, please let them get here in time.*

"I'm sorry, Amber. Thank you for all you've tried to do."

As Liv took aim, the door crashed inward.

Liv swung the weapon around and fired at the same time that Amber flung herself onto the bed and rolled. A second later she landed on the floor with a thud. Pain shot through her shoulder. A pillow lay on the floor beside her, apparently tossed aside by Liv during the night.

She looked under the bed. With nothing stored there, she had a clear view of the entire room, at least the lower few inches. Six feet away, Liv stood facing the door, weapon probably trained on the splintered opening. The only feet visible were hers. The deputy had apparently stayed in the hall.

"I have to do this." Conviction weighted the words. "I won't let you stop me. We both have to pay."

Liv fired off another shot. Amber watched her sidestep closer. Another shot rang out and she took a few more steps. She now stood less than three feet away, toenails painted in a playful design that didn't belong on the feet of a killer.

Another step brought Liv even closer. At any moment she'd move around the end of the bed and have a clear shot.

Amber looked frantically around for something with which to defend herself. The lamp on the nightstand was too far away and was likely plugged in. There was nothing under or beside the bed except the pillow.

Liv took another sideways step. Judging from the position of her feet, her attention was still on the door. It was now or never.

Amber snatched the pillow from the floor and sprang to her feet. In one smooth motion, she brought the pillow over her head and down on Liv's arm as Liv swung the weapon around.

The shot reverberated in the room. Caleb charged though the doorway and slammed into Liv, knocking her to the floor. The pistol skidded to a stop against the wall.

Amber grabbed it and looked around the room. Tiny feathers drifted downward to settle on the rumpled comforter, a hole blown through the fabric. Heavy footsteps pounded up the stairs. Then three deputies burst into the room. One unclipped a set of handcuffs from his belt and dropped to one knee beside Caleb, who had restrained Liv.

Liv twisted her head to the side and lifted her face from the floor, her eyes locking with Amber's. Tears streaked her cheeks. "Two more and the debt would have been paid. I was so close." She closed her eyes and dropped her head. "I'm sorry, Landon."

The deputy clicked the cuffs around Liv's wrists and helped her to her feet. Amber leaned against the windowsill, her legs suddenly ready to give out.

Caleb rose. He reached her in two large strides, wrapped her in his arms and held her as if he'd never let go. And she didn't want him to. She lifted her arms to embrace him and rested her face against his muscular chest.

Behind Caleb, one of the deputies was reading Liv her Miranda rights. Liv was surprisingly quiet.

Amber listened as footsteps retreated, through the doorway, down the hall and down the steps. And still Caleb held her.

Her eyes stung and she squeezed them shut. She was *not* going to cry. But the harder she tried to stop them, the more the tears came. Through everything, she'd held not only herself together but Liv, too. Now that it was no longer necessary, her innate inner strength had deserted her. Silent sobs shook her shoulders.

Caleb's grip tightened and he twisted her side to side in a soothing rocking motion. "Shh, it's okay. You're safe now." One hand came up to stroke her hair.

But the sobs wouldn't stop. She cried for Liv, whose miserable life had been doomed almost from birth. She cried for their friends, whose bad choices had sealed their deaths. And she cried for Landon, who hadn't done anything wrong and had lost his life to a lie.

Finally the sobs subsided, but Caleb didn't break the hug, so she didn't pull away, either. This was likely her last evening with him, so she was going to relish every moment.

It was over. In the morning, or maybe even tonight, she'd go back to Cedar Key. She'd return to her old life and Caleb would, too. Caleb wasn't interested in a relationship, with her or anyone. After tonight, their paths would likely never cross again.

The thought sent a pang into her heart as sharp as broken glass.

And every bit as painful.

TWELVE

Caleb tied off a plastic Walmart bag. Two others sat next to it, all three holding Olivia's possessions. Except the journal. The deputies had taken that into evidence.

When offered the choice between leaving or staying another night, Amber had been anxious to go home. At least to her temporary home with Hunter. Her own house wouldn't be livable for some time. If ever.

After sharing some pizza, they'd set about packing. The salad fixings he'd brought were sitting in the refrigerator, still in the bags.

Amber bent to pick up the pillow lying on the floor at the foot of the bed. "I'm afraid the comforter will need to be replaced. The mattress probably will, too." She tossed the pillow she held toward the headboard. "I think this pillow might have saved my life."

Caleb grinned. "I can't believe you defended yourself with a pillow."

"It gave me enough extended reach to deflect her shot until you could get inside and take her down." She shrugged, a grin quivering at the corner of her mouth. "Besides, I'm quite experienced with pillows as weapons. While you guys were doing campouts, us girls were having slumber parties, all of which included the obligatory pillow fight."

Caleb picked up the three bags sitting on the bed with one hand and Liv's purse with the other. "We'll locate Liv's family and try to get her stuff to them."

Amber nodded. "Her mother is pretty worthless, but I'm hoping her brother will step up. According to Liv, they've roomed together off and on. Some of the stuff at her house might even belong to him. I know the truck does."

After the deputies left, Amber had filled him in on everything. When she'd told him about the truck, the last piece of the puzzle had fallen into place. Liv had been slipping in and out of her house right under the noses of the deputies. Telling them she had the flu and was going to bed guaranteed they wouldn't question seeing no signs of movement inside the house.

Caleb headed toward the stairs, Amber walking ahead of him. Halfway there, she snagged some bags from the doorway of the other bedroom, those filled with her own items.

She stopped at the top of the stairs. "If her brother doesn't want her stuff, I suppose it'll be thrown away. No one else cares about her." She cast him a glance over her shoulder. "I plan to stay in touch."

Admiration swelled inside him, mixed with a hefty dose of amazement. Liv had just tried to kill her, but even that couldn't curb Amber's sympathetic nature. "You still want to help her, don't you?"

Amber started down the stairs. "Liv never had a chance. She was stuck with a mother who didn't want her and a series of stepfathers who considered her nothing but a big inconvenience. She spent her whole life looking for love and acceptance but never found it."

He followed, shaking his head. Amber was always thinking of those less fortunate. It was something they had in common. And something he loved about her.

She reached the foyer then watched him descend the final few steps. "In a desperate attempt to hold on to a shot at something special with Landon, she'd blurted out a lie that ended up getting him killed. The secret has eaten at her for the past ten years. When she reconnected with each of us and thought we'd all moved on with no regrets while she'd been racked with guilt, it pushed her over the edge."

Amber opened the front door and stepped onto the porch. "I hope she finds the help she needs."

After they'd loaded the items into Amber's SUV, they walked back toward the house. "I never did ask you how you knew something was up. I'd been racking my brain for a way to alert someone without getting shot, but couldn't come up with anything. When I heard someone sneaking up the stairs, I couldn't believe it."

Caleb led her inside. "On the way over here, I was mulling everything over in my mind, trying to think of something we'd overlooked. We were sure the killer was someone you all knew. He or she had to be an extremely good shot, too, to have killed the deputy in a moving vehicle. I remembered you saying Liv had competed in marksmanship and won tournaments. She's always seemed a little off, but lately it had gotten much worse."

He followed Amber into the family room where she began to put books into a bag. "Then I thought about her tattoo, the fact that she had a treble clef circling her initials even though she's never been involved in music. I remembered the treble clef Landon had drawn after his signature. One thought led to another and I questioned the *LC* she had tattooed on her back. I don't think it stood for Liv Chamberlain."

Amber straightened to look at him, her brows drawn together. "What else would—" Her eyes suddenly widened. "Landon Cleary."

He nodded. "It makes complete sense now that she's admitted to being in love with him."

Amber walked toward him with the bag of books. She'd kept one out. "I got two of these read and I'm half done with this one." She held up the single book. "I'd like to finish it, if you don't mind. I can return it to you when I'm through." Her gaze dipped to the floor. "Or, if you'd rather, I can take it directly to the library."

He shifted his weight from one foot to the other. Over the past hour they'd talked about all their hypotheses of the case, everything they'd pieced together and how good it felt for it to finally be over. The one thing they hadn't discussed was *What next?*

Frankly, he had no answer.

Amber handed him the bag, then brushed past him to cross the foyer. After laying the book on the living room coffee table, she picked up a stack of DVDs and stuffed them into another plastic bag. When she'd put away all the movies, she held up the sermon CD he'd loaned her. She was smiling.

He raised his brows. "Did you listen to it?"

"I did. I didn't think there'd be anything life-changing on here, but I figured if I listened, it would make you happy."

"And?"

"It tied right in with the sermon I'd heard at Hunter and Meagan's church last week. Everything finally clicked. Sometimes it takes three times to make a message hit home."

"What do you mean?"

"The great men of God who messed up."

"King David and Simon Peter. Who's the third?"

"Caleb Lyons." The smile she gave him was teasing but sincere. "I'm not sure the first two would have stuck without the third."

He matched her smile with one of his own, except his was bigger. Amber had finally found the peace and forgiveness she'd sought. And God had allowed him to play a part, however small.

He wrapped her in a hug and spun her in a full circle before once again placing her on her feet.

She draped her arms around his neck and looked up at him, joy lighting her eyes. "Thank you. For everything."

He tightened the embrace. She felt so good in his arms, so warm and soft. His gaze slid from her eyes to her lips, slightly parted and curved upward in a gentle smile.

More than anything, he wanted to kiss her. This time, he wanted it to be a real kiss, not an impulsive expression of relief. He didn't want it to be goodbye, either. He wanted it to be the start of forever. The realization shook him all the way to his toes.

Today he'd almost lost her. What would he have done then?

He released her and stepped away, everything he felt for her warring with the knowledge that in her line of work, her life could be snuffed out in an instant.

He cleared his throat. "Let's get the last of the stuff loaded."

She drew in a shaky breath and gave a sharp nod.

When he stepped out the front door, the sky at the end of the driveway was ablaze with color. But it didn't inspire the usual awe in him. His heart was too troubled.

Two more trips inside had all of the food loaded. They'd split the leftover pizza and he'd given the salad items to Amber. The final trip, they collected Tippy, her dishes and her litter box.

She closed the SUV door and turned to face him.

He rested a hand on her shoulder. "Take care of yourself."

"You, too. Can we stay in touch?"

He hesitated. Cutting ties with her would be like taking a razor blade to his heart. But he wouldn't make promises he couldn't keep.

"I need time."

She nodded and sadness settled in her eyes, shredding his already raw emotions.

He watched her climb into the SUV then walked to his truck. He'd said he needed time.

Time for what? To decide he was ready to set aside his fears of losing her and take a chance on love?

He closed the door. No, that wasn't it at all. He needed time to distance himself from all that had transpired over the past four weeks.

Eventually everything he felt for her would fade.

And she'd be nothing more than a bittersweet memory.

Amber cruised down Highway 19, headed toward Chiefland. She'd spent the evening a short distance north of there, playing rummy with Mr. Gaines, one of her hospice patients.

She'd be arriving at Hunter's an hour later than planned. After Mrs. Gaines had finished her birthday dinner out with family, she'd insisted that Amber enjoy the leftover cake she'd brought home.

Sitting with Mr. Gaines was always a pleasure. Though he wasn't looking forward to the dying process, he was ready and eagerly anticipating Heaven. The circumstances were never easy, but those with a strong faith almost always fared better than those without.

She eased to a stop and waited for a traffic light to change. Tippy was going to be happy to see her when she got home. She'd adjusted well to Meagan's studio, and there hadn't been any incidents since Liv had let her out three weeks ago.

Amber stepped on the gas, her heart singing. It was good to be doing most of the things she'd done before. In fact, it was even better. There was nothing like experiencing the simple joy of service, as Caleb had put it, without the concern that no matter what she did, it wouldn't be enough.

Tonight the only thing dampening her spirit was Caleb. She'd hoped to hear from him within a few days after leaving his aunt and uncle's place. But when a few days stretched into a week, she'd given up hope. Tomorrow was going to be two weeks, and she hadn't spoken to him since saying goodbye in front of the old farmhouse.

She drove though the last traffic light heading out of Chiefland. Caleb lived a few blocks away. He'd told her the name of his road, but even though he'd been to her house several times, she'd never been to his.

She heaved a sigh. He'd done so much for her. It wasn't just the work on the case and everything he'd done to protect her. His testimony had transformed her life. For the first time in over a decade, she was free.

And he was still bound.

The sad irony struck her with the force of a lightning bolt.

After glancing in the rearview mirror, she jammed on the brakes and made a sharp right. She couldn't help Caleb if he wasn't willing to be helped. But she had to try.

She made a couple of turns, then drove slowly down a small street, straining to identify the makes and models of the vehicles sitting in the driveways. This would be much easier in daylight. But if she waited, she'd lose her courage.

Ahead on the right was a dark F-150. She drew to a stop under a nearby streetlight. Extended cab. Same body style. It could definitely be Caleb's.

She pulled in behind it and stepped from her vehicle. When she rang the bell, a dog barked. Another good sign. Caleb had a dog.

The door swung open. Caleb's eyes widened then narrowed as several emotions flitted across his face. Amid the confusion and surprise, had there been a flicker of joy? Was he a little happy to see her?

"What are you doing here?" His voice wasn't cold but it held undeniable tension.

Okay, maybe not. She squared her shoulders. She wouldn't chicken out now.

"We need to talk. May I come in?"

After several seconds' hesitation he opened the door wider, but he didn't offer her a seat.

A beagle mix approached, wagging its tail. A cat peered at her from the arm of a recliner. When no introduction was forthcoming, she bent to pet the dog.

Finally she straightened. Caleb stood watching her, jaw tight. He wasn't going to make this easy.

She resisted the urge to wring her hands. She also dismissed the idea of making small talk. Anything she asked would likely garner single-word answers.

She drew in a deep breath. "You helped me find freedom. I'm here to return the favor."

"What are you talking about?"

"Your wife was murdered. That was horrible beyond words. I can't even begin to imagine what you went through. But it's been four years and you're still letting it dictate your life."

He crossed his arms and turned away, offering her his shoulder. "You don't know what you're talking about."

"I know hurt when I see it. And I know fear. What is fear, except lack of trust?"

She moved to stand in front of him, but he refused to look at her.

"Come on, Caleb. I want to know where the faith is that you always talk about having."

His eyes met hers but they held disdain rather than warmth. "You've been a Christian for what, two weeks, and you're judging *me*?"

She chose to ignore the barb. "You say you trust God. Is your faith strong enough to believe God will take care of me?" When he didn't respond, she continued. "More importantly, is it strong enough to believe, in the event of the unthinkable, that God will take care of *you*?"

She stared up at him, waiting for a response, even a nonverbal one. She got nothing. He stood stock-still, his gaze fixed on a point over her head. She heaved a sigh, her shoulders slumping with the motion. She wasn't good at one-sided conversations.

"Think about what I said." She stepped around him and walked toward the front door. With her hand resting on the knob, she turned and spoke to his back. "I love you, Caleb. And I believe you feel something for me. But if you're going to live your life bound up with fear, you'll never experience all God has for you."

She swung open the door and stepped into the night. For years, she'd filled her life with work and her volunteer activities, not allowing herself time to even think about romance.

Then out of the blue, God had thrown Caleb in her path. Was his only purpose in her life to get her on the right road? Or did God have more for them?

She was sure it was the latter.

She climbed into the RAV4 and started the engine.

God, I've done all I can do. I'm leaving it in your hands.

She shook her head. Talk about trust.

Caleb plopped into his recliner and put his head in his hands. Amber showing up on his doorstep had knocked the foundation from under him.

He didn't invite women into his home. It set up too many unreasonable expectations. And brought back too many memories.

He'd told her he needed time. And she'd come anyway.

Kira approached and nudged his hand away from his face. He lifted his head and scratched her under the chin.

It had been two weeks. And he was no closer to forgetting Amber than when he'd watched the RAV4 roll down his aunt and uncle's driveway.

What he'd done hadn't been fair to Amber. She'd asked if they'd see each other again and he'd left her hanging. He should tell her to forget about him. Make a clean break. But he wasn't ready to do that, either.

"What do I do, Kira?"

Tess head-butted his other arm, demanding attention, also. He dragged a hand down her silky back and contented purrs rumbled through her body.

He'd finally reached a point where he was willing to consider a relationship with the woman God had for him. As long as she wasn't a cop.

At the last thought, he cringed. Obedience had no conditions. Any commitment beginning with *I will obey if…*wasn't true obedience. Could he, in all truthfulness, tell God he was ready, without qualifying it?

He rose and strode into the kitchen. Kira and Tess followed. Ignoring their hopeful eyes, he walked to the living room then retraced his steps.

Amber had said he had trust issues. He hadn't wanted to hear it, but she was right. He didn't fully trust God. If he did, he wouldn't be holding back.

But he didn't trust himself, either. He'd already failed once. Why would he think the next time would be any different? But wasn't it a lack of trust in God, also, doubting that He'd give him the strength to weather whatever storms he faced?

Amber was right about something else, too. She'd said she believed he cared for her. He did. More than he had for anyone in a long time.

He hadn't wanted to. He'd fought it. But as he'd spent time with her and witnessed her sweet nature and giving spirit, he'd quickly lost the battle.

For two weeks he'd tried to douse what had developed between them. It hadn't worked. He was in love with her. There was no sense denying it.

He snatched his keys from the end table and strode toward the door. He needed to see Amber. But first he needed to have a long talk with God. The thirty-minute drive would give him that opportunity.

When he crossed the last bridge onto Cedar Key a half hour later, it was with a much lighter heart. He'd worked through a lot and couldn't wait to tell Amber. But when he pulled into Hunter's driveway, the house was dark except for the bulb burning on the front porch. Amber couldn't be asleep. He was only a half hour behind her.

He pulled out his phone and dialed her number. She answered on the first ring. Her hello was hesitant but her sweet voice warmed him inside.

"Am I calling too late?"

"No. I'm getting ready for bed."

"That's what I thought. The house is dark."

"You're here?"

He smiled at the surprise in her tone. Or maybe it was excitement. He climbed from the truck and headed toward the porch.

A light came on behind the vertical blinds. Then the dead bolt clicked. A second later the door swung open. Amber stood there with red-rimmed eyes.

His heart twisted. She'd been crying. And he'd caused those tears.

"What are you doing here?"

Her words were the same ones he'd said to her earlier.

"We need to talk. May I come in?" They'd just switched roles.

She invited him inside and motioned toward the living room couch. "Have a seat."

He winced. She had the better manners. He deserved to be left standing in the foyer.

When he sat, she sank down next to him and he took her hand.

"Thank you for stopping to talk to me. Your speech about trust was spot-on. I'm sorry I didn't accept it right away. I can be hard-headed sometimes."

She squeezed his hand. "You're a guy. It's to be expected."

He gave her a crooked smile. "Thanks."

"I'm glad it made you think."

"It did more than that. I had a long talk with God on the way over here."

"An argument?"

"Not this time. I've done enough of that the past four weeks. I'm through fighting what's been developing between us. I still go crazy when I think about you responding to a call or even going on your early morning run alone, but I'm ready to give this thing a try."

He turned so he could face her more fully and took her other hand. "I love you, Amber. And now I'd like to do something I've been wanting to do ever since you gave me the victory hug at your uncle's archery tournament."

"And what might that be?" Her eyes danced, telling him she already knew the answer.

He released her hands to cup her face. As he leaned toward her, her eyes drifted closed and he slid one hand back to entwine his fingers in her hair.

As soon as his lips met hers, her arms encircled his neck, encouraging him to deepen the kiss. Warmth flowed through him, banishing the loneliness that had plagued him for the past four years and fulfilling every longing he'd ever had.

This was the Amber he loved. She didn't do anything halfway. Her passion and enthusiasm showed in everything she did. As long as he was with her, he'd never doubt her love for him.

When he finally broke the kiss, a smile of contentment spread across her face. ""Tis better to have loved and lost than never to have loved at all.'"

"I agree wholeheartedly."

"Who said that?"

"Alfred Lord Tennyson."

Her smile widened. "You always were too smart for your own good."

"I might be smart, but it took you to open my eyes."

"That proves we make a good team."

A team. It had a nice sound. "Two are better than one. If they fall, one will lift the other up. Though one can be defeated, two can defend themselves."

"Is that something Jesus said?"

"Solomon, loosely paraphrased." He squeezed her hands. "I can't think of anyone I'd rather have on my team."

She completed him and he completed her. Together they found freedom.

God had given him a precious gift and because it wasn't on his own terms, he'd almost walked away.

He pulled her back into his arms and offered up a silent prayer of thanks. Instead of a life of loneliness, he was looking forward to a future with Amber.

A future bright with promise.

A future filled with love.

* * * * *

If you enjoyed this exciting story of suspense and intrigue, pick up these other stories from Carol J. Post:

SHATTERED HAVEN
HIDDEN IDENTITY
MISTLETOE JUSTICE
BURIED MEMORIES

Available now from Love Inspired Suspense!

Find more great reads at
www.LoveInspired.com

Dear Reader,

I hope you've enjoyed our final trip to Cedar Key. I'm a little sad to leave our friends there. It's one of my favorite places to visit, with its quaint, artsy atmosphere and friendly people.

I've had fun bringing you Amber and Caleb's story. Amber grew up under the shadow of a "perfect" older brother and never felt as if she was good enough. She made some serious mistakes and carried some heavy regrets. After years of trying to earn God's forgiveness, she finally realized grace isn't something that can be earned; it is offered freely through Christ's sacrifice.

Amber saw Caleb as "super Christian," but he was carrying regrets. He'd always thought he had a strong faith, but when it was tested, he failed miserably. Though he found his way back, the road to complete trust in God was a long one. I hope one or both of these characters' struggles spoke to you.

I would love it if you'd drop me a line. You can find me on Facebook at www.Facebook.com/caroljpost.author and on Twitter @caroljpost, or visit my website www.caroljpost.com and email me at caroljpost@gmail.com.

For news and fun contests, join my newsletter. The link is on my website. I promise I won't sell your info or spam you!

God bless you!
Carol